SUMMER
OF THE
DODO

SUMMER

O F   T H E

DODO

PATRICIA
BAEHR

Harcourt Brace Jovanovich, Inc.
Orlando Austin San Diego Chicago Dallas New York

As a part of the HBJ TREASURY OF LITERATURE, 1993 Edition, this edition is published by special arrangement with Four Winds Press, an imprint of Macmillan Publishing Company.

Grateful acknowledgment is made to Four Winds Press, an imprint of Macmillan Publishing Company for permission to reprint *Summer of the Dodo* by Patricia Baehr. Copyright © 1990 by Patricia Goehner Baehr.

Cover illustration copyright © 1990 by Eileen McKeating

Printed in the United States of America

ISBN 0-15-300360-X

1 2 3 4 5 6 7 8 9 10   059   96   95   94   93   92

For

PETER

and

GEMMA

CONTENTS

CHAPTER 1

DODO AND ARLEY

What was so wrong with worms?

Dodo Penny pondered that question on the third step of the Penny front stoop, her tongue stuck out as far as it would go in order to see just how thin she had sucked a peppermint Lifesaver.

"Got one for me, Dodo?"

Arley, her younger brother, sat down beside her. Dodo snapped her tongue back into her mouth as if it were a window shade someone had pulled. She shook her head. She wasn't talking to Arley. It had been his idea to rescue the worms in the first place.

"They're dying!" he had urged her. "After the rain last night, they were all flooded from their houses. If we don't pick them out of the puddles, they'll *die*!"

Houses! As if worms built houses or could care whether or not they drowned.

"That's absolutely, positively the last stunt you'll talk me into, Arley," she announced, poking out her elbows and knees to take up as much room as possible on the step. "And I've told you a ka-jillion times, stop calling me *Dodo!*"

Her given name was Dorothy, but no one at home called her that.

"Dodo sounds babyish. It sounds dumb," she argued, not for the first time. "If you ever let on in school that my name is anything but Dorothy, I'll— I'll do something awful!"

Summer vacation had just started, but already Dodo was dreading the fall, when Arley would move up to the fourth grade and the middle school. Dodo's school.

"I know what I'll do," she said with sudden inspiration. "I'll flush one piece out of each of your jigsaw puzzles down the toilet!"

For a moment Arley looked horrified. Then, as he picked up a stone and began to chip at the cement step, his face relaxed. "You wouldn't dare. And besides, I didn't call you anything when those girls stopped."

Dodo groaned. In her mind, she could still see the expressions on the faces of the Big Three. They *would* come along as she was saving the fattest, longest, wiggliest worm of all.

"What are you doing?" Gigi Bell had asked.

Arley had piped an answer before Dodo could think. "We're saving lives."

"Saving *worms'* lives?"

Watching Barbie Fishbein's eyebrows arch into

disbelief, Dodo had done the first thing to pop into her head: she'd flung the creature dangling from her fingers onto the lawn behind her. She was sure things would have been all right if Arley hadn't over-reacted, screaming that she was a murderer before running off to find the worm. To Dodo's dismay, Tamara Hughes had murmured a quick good-bye, and then all three of the girls had continued on down the street.

It was Barbie Fishbein who had dubbed the girls the Big Three. They were always together, at lunch, at assembly, on the playground. They picked each other for teams in gym and slept over each other's houses on weekends. To Dodo, who often found herself standing alone outside school, waiting for the bell to sound, they had the perfect arrangement, and she would have gladly changed it to the Big Four: Gigi, Barbie, Tamara, *and Dodo.*

And *Dorothy,* she mentally corrected herself, cracking the paper-thin candy between her tongue and the roof of her mouth.

Of course, that was the first strike against her. Even if everyone at school did call her Dorothy, she still thought of herself as Dodo. Silly, babyish, always-say-the-wrong-thing Dodo. She slid down to the second step of the stoop to be farther away from her brother. If he had been a smart baby, able to pronounce her name properly, no one ever would have started calling her Dodo.

"Hey!" Arley complained as she popped another Lifesaver into her mouth. "I thought you didn't have any more."

Dodo ignored him. Any of the Big Three would have known touching worms was *out*, she thought. But that was the second strike against her. Dodo never realized what was *out* until after she'd already done it.

"Make way," Aunt Hazel Penny sang, coming out of the front door with two blankets, two pillows, and a wide-brimmed straw hat in her arms. She was a tall woman, thin, with freckles and a very straight spine. Her reddish brown hair fluffed out around her head, as untamed as a lion's mane. Aunt Hazel was the person Dodo had taken after in appearance.

The third strike against me, Dodo thought. Whenever she remembered the fact that she was a full head taller than any of the Big Three, she hunched over and tried to squash down her hair. Three strikes and you were *out*. Out, out, OUT!

"Got to finish packing the car," Aunt Hazel said. "Want to be there in time for dinner. You know, I haven't been to my little place in over a year." As she folded herself in half to arrange the provisions in the back seat of her tiny car, Aunt Hazel exclaimed, "I do love vacations!"

To Dodo's way of thinking, Aunt Hazel was always on vacation. Traveling was her job. She collected

4

specimens for museums, and it seemed to Dodo a good kind of job to have. Aunt Hazel was always having adventures, and she had learned just about everything there was to learn. She knew where to find dinosaur bones and when there would be meteor showers; she knew how to cook blubber and how to dance for rain.

"You kids be sure to behave for Aunt Hazel," Mrs. Penny said from the front door. With her sandy-colored hair and classic features, Mrs. Penny was the good-looking one in the family. And it appeared, to Dodo's chagrin, that Arley was going to take after her.

"Daddy and I will keep in touch by phone," she promised, bringing out the family's battered suitcase. It was the only one they had, the one Mr. Penny took on business trips, the one that, up until yesterday, had stored Arley's Lego sets. "You be sure to brush your teeth every day and to change your underwear. And eat whatever Aunt Hazel puts in front of you—"

"What if she gives me an orange?" Arley interrupted. He was allergic to oranges.

"No. Don't eat oranges," Mrs. Penny said, revising her statement. "Eat everything else."

"What if she gives me something that's rotten?" Arley persisted.

"Well, of course I wouldn't expect you to eat anything that had gone bad, Arley. Eat everything but oranges and rotten food."

"What if it's poisoned?"

"But your aunt wouldn't give you anything that was poisoned—"

Aunt Hazel winked at Dodo. "Don't know about that. Lost a cat once. Never did find out what happened to it. Always suspected it might have been the chicken livers I gave it."

"I don't like chicken livers," Arley warned. "They taste like dirt."

Mrs. Penny started down the steps, the weight of the suitcase making her crooked. "I hope you'll be all right, Hazel. You're not used to children. At times they can be . . ." She hesitated, searching for the right word.

"Trying," Arley supplied for her.

Aunt Hazel took the suitcase and lifted it onto the top of her car with ease. "Haven't met a situation yet that I couldn't handle," she said, using a rope to tie everything in place. "We'll be just fine. My bungalow is near the water. They'll have the sand and the waves to play in, lots of space to explore, and plenty of animals to study. Fish, crabs, heron, sea gulls . . ."

Would the Big Three play and explore and study animals? Dodo smiled. It didn't matter, anyway. There was an entire summer separating her from

September and sixth grade and worries about whether she was *in* or *out*.

"There!" Aunt Hazel announced. "All set. Kiss your mother good-bye, kids, and get into the car!"

CHAPTER 2

><>

THE
BUNGALOW

". . . and pass it around, no more bottles of pop on the wall!"

Dodo sighed. Aunt Hazel was the only person she knew who started the singing at *five hundred* bottles of *pop* on the wall. It had taken at least sixty miles to finish the song. Arley's complaints at the length of the drive had prompted Aunt Hazel's performance, but he had had the nerve to fall asleep in the back seat when they'd taken down bottle number three hundred forty-four.

"Almost there."

"Good," Dodo said, sitting up straighter to look out the window. She couldn't see the Sound. She knew it was supposed to be a very large body of water emptying into the Atlantic Ocean, but the only moisture around was the sweat running down her back. It was very warm in Aunt Hazel's car. For some reason, just the driver's window could be opened.

"Here is the Long Island Sound," she imagined

herself saying to the Big Three. They would be riding in a spacious new car, of course, not a used compact, driven by a handsome chauffeur instead of Aunt Hazel. How impressed Gigi, Barbie, and Tamara would be. Directed by Dodo, they would step out onto an enormous, pristine beach of white—no, *pink*—sand, and ooh and aah at the giant swells of sparkling water.

"Better wake up your brother," Aunt Hazel said, breaking into Dodo's daydream. "Going to need him to help carry things into the bungalow."

Dodo shifted in her seat to reach Arley's sneaker. She grabbed it and shook.

"No more bottles," he moaned.

"Wake up. You're going to have to carry things into the bungalow."

Bungalow. It was funny to say. Bungalow, bungalow, Dodo mouthed silently. It gave her tongue a strange feeling, the way cooked celery did when her mother managed to sneak it into a soup. She scraped the length of her tongue along her top front teeth. What exactly was a bungalow?

"This is where we'll be staying," Dodo said, back with the Big Three. In her mind, she stood the four of them before a quaint cottage set smack in the middle of the beach and surrounded by roses and a white picket fence. All of its windows had window seats and were open to catch the breeze off the water.

"Where *is* the water?" Dodo wanted to know, returning her attention to the heat and noise of the car. Outside were fields and houses hiding behind trees.

Aunt Hazel didn't answer right away. She steered along the snakelike turns of the road, finally replying, "Patience is a virtue." Almost immediately, they left the trees behind them, and a blue shimmer appeared on the horizon.

"Yippee!" Arley exclaimed, coming to life in the back seat amid the linens and pillows. "Can you stop the car and let us go down and get our feet wet?"

Dodo stared. The beach was a fairly narrow strip, comprised of what appeared to be stones sprouting umbrellas. The waves were no grander than any she might create in the bathtub. The sounds came not from the surf but from radios and people, people of all shapes and sizes and shades of tan.

In her imagination, Dodo heard Gigi sigh.

"Come on, Tamara," Barbie called. *"Gigi and I are going back to my house."*

"Good-bye, Dorothy," Tamara said.

"That's the public beach," Aunt Hazel stated, as if she could hear the Big Three as clearly as Dodo could. "Our beach is private."

"Are we close by?" Arley asked.

"Very," Aunt Hazel confirmed.

Pizzeria. Video arcade. Miniature golf. Ice cream

parlor. A restaurant called Davy Jones's Locker. The buildings sat opposite the beach, a wooden board-walk connecting them. Nowhere could Dodo see the beautiful cottage.

"This is where we leave the car," Aunt Hazel said, pulling up the parking brake on what should have been the lawn of a large, dilapidated house. The lot was mostly dirt, though, and had been rutted by tires. "Hop out, now. I'll untie the suitcases and unload the car. You two go down and open up the bungalow. It's the third one on the right, counting back from the beach."

"I see the water! I see the water!" Key in hand, Arley ran down a slope beside the house that seemed to serve as some kind of lane between smaller houses.

Bungalows, Dodo thought, scraping her tongue against her teeth again as she followed him. They were nearly identical: small, low buildings with porches in front. The only difference was that some of the porches were open, while some were screened in and still others were enclosed with plastic.

"Wait up!" she called.

Arley didn't hear her. He'd reached the bottom of the incline where the lane looped around an old oak tree. Dodo watched as he threw himself against a stone seawall there. He paused only long enough to take in the view, then disappeared to the left.

"Arley!" As Dodo shouted, her eye was caught by a movement behind the plastic-covered screens of one of the bungalows. Turning her head, she saw a curtain being hurriedly closed. "We're supposed to unlock Aunt Hazel's house," she called ahead to her brother, "not go off exploring—"

At the oak, Dodo stopped to gaze at what lay before her, beyond the seawall. Boats. Hazy blue expanse of sea and sky. Birds with their feathers blazing in the lowering sun. *Shwump, shwump* of waves curling here, there, here again, all at once breaking in one long line. *SHWUMP.* It was peaceful. It was beautiful, not in a grand pink-sand way, but beautiful nonetheless.

The Big Three returned to Dodo's imagination. *"Dorothy knows how to swim,"* Gigi said, a smile on her lips.

"She can teach us," Barbie added.

"What are you doing here?" asked Tamara.

Tamara wasn't supposed to say that. Dodo shook her head roughly.

"Did you hear me, Dorothy? I said, what are you doing here?"

To the left of the seawall was a wooden staircase leading to the beach. At its summit stood Tamara Hughes.

"Rudolfo will serve dinner at seven," Dodo said, surprised at how well her imagination worked.

Looking confused, Tamara pulled a towel snug around her. Without Gigi and Barbie flanking her, she seemed even smaller than usual. Dodo automatically rounded her own shoulders and put her hands up to flatten her hair.

"I guess I'll see you around, Dorothy."

Amazed, Dodo watched Tamara pass her and head up the lane. She was *here.* Really and truly. Tamara Hughes, one third of the Big Three. Maybe this was Dodo's chance to become the Big Fourth!

"Come on!" she shouted to Arley jubilantly. He was running in the gentle wash of the waves, still wearing his shoes. "Bring the key and let's open up the bungalow!"

———

"One," Arley counted, his sneakers squishing with every step. "Two. Three. This is Aunt Hazel's bunga-whatsit."

Dodo hesitated. The building before them was the one where the curtain had moved. She was sure of it. She counted for herself. The third bungalow from the beach. When Aunt Hazel said right, did she mean it would be on their right when they were facing the water or on their right when they faced the car?

Arley had already let himself onto the porch. He jingled Aunt Hazel's key chain importantly.

"Does the key fit?" Dodo asked, rushing onto the porch to join him.

In answer, he swung the door open, letting a blast of words escape.

"—*This offer is not available in any store. You would have to travel to Europe to find the kind of craftsmanship and quality*—"

Dodo grabbed Arley's collar and pulled him back. "This is the wrong place!"

"The key fit."

"—*Our operators are standing by. Dial one eight hundred*—"

"What's going on here? Who turned on the TV?" Aunt Hazel pushed past them, then froze.

The bungalow lay in violent disarray. Books, statues, and other odd items from Aunt Hazel's travels were strewn about. Empty cans littered the floor. One couch cushion had been moved into the middle of the room and ripped open. Its stuffing protruded like some artificial nest.

With one swift movement, Aunt Hazel spun around and swept both children out of the house and into the lane. Setting them a safe distance from the bungalow, she proceeded to knock at an adjacent door to ask that 911 be dialed.

Perched beside her brother on some paving stones edging the tiny neighboring garden, Dodo watched until a police car rolled down the narrow path. When two officers got out, one approached Aunt Hazel, while the other walked around the perimeter of her bungalow.

"What seems to be the problem, ma'am?"

"Someone has broken into my summer home," Aunt Hazel explained. "Might still be there. Television is on. I think I heard water running in the kitchen."

Dodo was impressed by her aunt's calmness. The people gathering around the car were clucking their tongues, acting more upset than Aunt Hazel.

"Possible burglary in process," the first policeman said to a third, who had arrived in another car. Putting his hand on the butt of the gun in his holster, he called, "Stay out here. We'll search inside."

"I hope they shoot him!" Arley crowed. When Aunt Hazel turned and eyed him severely, he added, "Not dead. I don't even care if they miss. I just want to hear a gun go off."

It was several minutes before the officer who had spoken to Aunt Hazel emerged again. Dodo was wondering if Tamara was in one of the bungalows on the lane and if she had noticed the commotion.

"Somebody's been here, that's for sure," the policeman said. "It's a real mess inside. But we searched every room, and the place is empty now."

"Where did they break in?"

"No sign of forced entry, ma'am. The door must have been opened somehow."

"It was locked when I got to it," Arley volunteered.

"You just thought it was, son," the officer said. "There's nobody in there. And no burglar that I ever heard of locked a door behind him when he left."

"But I heard a click when I turned the key!" Arley insisted.

The policeman smiled tolerantly at Aunt Hazel. "Why don't you check for damage."

"Disturbance at Ransom Beach. See complainant with inflated sea horse."

Hearing the call come over the radio, the third policeman headed for his car. Aunt Hazel strode onto the bungalow porch with Dodo and Arley on her heels. "Porch seems untouched," she stated.

It wasn't that easy to see. The sun was dipping down behind the bungalows across the way and could only dimly penetrate the plastic over the screens. Dodo's eyes picked out a set of lawn chairs, a pair of oars, a pile of life jackets, a folded beach umbrella, a bag of charcoal, and a round barbecue on three legs. She decided it had been some trick of light from the setting sun that had made her think she saw a curtain move.

In the living room, the second officer was bouncing a flat-topped rock in his hand, his attention momentarily caught by the courtroom scene depicted on the television. "Did you ever see a witness confess to the crime on the stand?" he asked Aunt Hazel. "I never have. To watch this stuff, you'd think it happened every day."

When Aunt Hazel said nothing, the policeman leaned forward to shut off the set and spoke briskly.

"In this case, I'll bet it was kids. See how they left garbage and empty soup cans and rocks all over the place? Looks just like my kids' room at home."

As he prepared to heave the stone out the door, Aunt Hazel sprang at him. "Don't! That's my Burgess Shale trilobite."

Dodo remembered Aunt Hazel's tale of fossil hunting on a mountain trail in Canada. After a tumble which had left one of her feet dangling over the edge of a cliff, Aunt Hazel had discovered the outlines of sea creatures that had existed hundreds of millions of years ago.

"Oh, sure. Trilobite," the policeman said. "I thought that's what it was."

The other policeman cleared his throat. "Does anything appear to be missing? We ought to be moving on to that sea horse case."

"Of course," Aunt Hazel murmured, and as Dodo and Arley watched, she examined the remaining rooms.

It didn't take very long. There were only four total, all of them small: the living room, a bedroom, a kitchen, and a dining room that doubled as a hallway, doorways in three of its walls and a table against the fourth. The furniture in the place looked secondhand, or at least much used. It went along perfectly with the bungalow's rather run-down appearance. Floors buckled. Window glass rippled. Curtains hung limp. Dodo's impression of the kitchen was that it was a closet outfitted with ancient appliances. The bathroom squeezed between it and the bedroom was a telephone booth with shower stall, sink, and toilet.

"This egg that I thought was petrified seems to have been smashed," Aunt Hazel said, fingering a large piece of broken shell. "All the cupboards and closets have been ransacked, but nothing seems to be missing— Wait. My pheasant."

"Is this it, ma'am?" one of the policemen asked. He held up a rather motley stuffed bird by one of its tail feathers.

"That's it. Where was it?"

"Garbage can in the kitchen."

"That'll account for the feathers all over," the second policeman said.

The feathers on the bird were brown and gold, Dodo noted. The ones on the furniture and floor were ash colored.

"Near as I can tell," the first policeman said, "your only loss was food. And the broken egg. Where did you keep that egg, ma'am?"

Dodo picked up an empty can of pork and beans. The lid looked as though it had been pierced by some primitive sort of can opener.

"On the television set," Aunt Hazel answered.

"Want to make up a complaint?"

"No, no," Aunt Hazel said wearily. "We'll never find out who did this. I just wonder how long ago they left. The least they could have done was turn off the TV. Do you suppose it's been on all year?"

"Your electric bill should tell you that," one of the officers said as he headed for the door. "You have a good day, now!"

The day was nearly over, Dodo realized. The only thing good about it had been the presence of Tamara. Consoling herself with that thought, she helped Arley bring the suitcases and boxes from the car.

———

After an attempt at organizing the rooms and a lick-and-promise cleaning, Aunt Hazel made supper from the food they had brought with them.

"There are three kinds of fruit juices to choose from," she said as they sat down around the yellow Formica-topped table.

Immediately, Arley gulped down two cups of juice and helped himself to a peanut butter and banana sandwich, but Dodo could muster little interest in eating. "Where do we sleep?" she asked with a yawn.

"We'll share the bedroom, Dodo, and let Arley have the couch. I've turned the damaged cushion over, stuffed some towels under it—"

Arley's foot was tapping at the table leg. *Tap tap tap tap.*

"—it'll have to do for now. As soon as we've eaten, let's call it bedtime," Aunt Hazel finished.

"I'm not tired," Arley announced. *Tap tap tap tap.* Dodo managed to lift up her head so that she could look into her brother's eyes. They were abnormally bright. "What kind of juice did you drink?" she demanded.

Tap tap tap tap, went Arley's foot. "I don't know. This one."

"You big dope," Dodo cried. "That's orange juice! You know you're allergic!"

"Allergic?" Aunt Hazel echoed.

"Mom didn't mention orange *juice,*" Arley explained. *Tap tap.* "She only said not to eat oranges and rotten food and—"

"He'll be up for hours," Dodo told her aunt. "That's the way it affects him."

Tap tap tap tap.

"Go on to bed," Aunt Hazel told Dodo. "I'll stay up with Einstein!"

CHAPTER 3

━━━

THE
INTRUDER

"Psst. Are the cops gone?"

Hearing the voice, Dodo rolled into a hollow in the middle of Aunt Hazel's double bed. The room was dark, but with the door ajar, and light emanating from the television, she could see the dim outlines of the highboy and the room's one window. Five minutes to twelve, she read on Aunt Hazel's travel clock.

"What show's next?" Arley was asking Aunt Hazel in the living room.

When she spoke, Aunt Hazel's voice sounded hopeful. "Tired?"

Dodo heard a muffled thumping, the kind of noise a sneaker would make against a couch. "Nope," said Arley.

The voice must have come from the TV, Dodo thought, moving back to her own side of the bed. Funny. It had sounded so close.

"Psst. Is it safe to come out now?"

The voice had not come from the television. It had

come from under the bed. The intruder! Dodo sat up fast and pulled the sheet to her chin.

"Can't you talk?" the voice asked in a hoarse whisper.

"Of course I can," Dodo said, wondering why she was whispering in return. "Whoever you are, get out of here fast or I'll *scream.*"

"Don't scream, don't scream," the voice pleaded.

There were scuffing noises as the intruder struggled to move out from under the bed. Dodo closed her eyes, not wanting to see, but she quickly opened them again. Not to see would be worse. In the dimness, the intruder looked like a lump standing or kneeling or sitting just beyond the foot of the bed.

"My, but you're large!" the lump said. *"Huge,* in fact."

Dodo pressed her sleep-tousled hair close to her head, for the moment forgetting her alarm. "From what I can see, you look as fat as a beach ball, so I wouldn't be calling people huge if I were you."

When the intruder moved toward the door, there was a curious clicking on the linoleum. For a moment, he—or she or it—was silhouetted in the wash of blue light cast by the television, and it looked to Dodo as if there were something sharp sticking out from the head. Before she could get a good look, though, the intruder closed the door, putting them in near total darkness.

"Get out!" Dodo hissed in fright.

"Turn on the lamp."

Thinking that whoever it was would seem less frightening if she could see, Dodo obeyed.

"You look just like the people in the box, only much bigger."

Unaccustomed to the light, Dodo's eyes took an unbearable number of seconds to focus on the creature in Aunt Hazel's bedroom. "You're a bird!" she gasped.

The intruder stretched out two tiny wings sporting whitish feathers. "Oh, do you think so? Fifty bonus points for you and a home version of our game!"

If it was a bird, it was a preposterous one, Dodo decided. It had a huge, globular body covered with blue-gray feathers, a large head, an enormous black beak, and yellow legs that, although stout, seemed hardly capable of supporting the creature's weight. For a few moments, she watched as the being wiggled some curly feathers that sat high on its rear end.

"What people? What box?" she asked finally, remembering what the bird had said.

"The box with the shows. You know. Game shows, comedy shows, police shows."

Dodo understood. "The television."

"Yes, that's what it's called. I knew what people would look like, but I had no idea they would be *this* big. You all look so small and flat on the television. And so much plainer."

"Aunt Hazel's TV is black and white."

"Black and white. I don't know what that means," the bird said.

"Some sets have color," Dodo explained. "Like the colors you see around—" She stopped as a thought occurred to her. "You ate the food," she said. "You're the one who wrecked the house."

The bird pecked at the seam in the linoleum with its hooked bill, chipping off a piece of a flower in the floor's design. "I meant to clean up. I never expected company. You didn't give me any warning at all." It stood up straight again. "I hope you've brought more food."

"We did."

"Pattycake Cakes?" The feathers on the tail seemed to quiver. "Twinkle Pies and Crumbly Crumbs and Fruitsters? Nice mothers give their families Pattycake Cakes."

Dodo shook her head in amazement. "Where did you come from?"

"From?"

"Yes. Where were you before you broke into Aunt Hazel's bungalow?"

The bird's tiny eyes seemed to glaze over. "Bungalow? I don't know that word. Pass."

"Pass?"

"Yes. Give me the next clue, please."

"There are no clues."

"You mean I don't win?"

"Look," Dodo started again, determined to learn something. "You had to have come from someplace. Where were you born?"

"Born?"

"Yes. You know. When you came out of your egg. Your mother must have been there—"

The bird was shaking its head. Suddenly, as it looked at Dodo, its eyes brightened.

"I'm not your mother," Dodo told it, reading its expression. "What's the first thing you remember?"

"The box," the bird said, seeming happy at being able to answer a question.

"But you couldn't have been hatched here in Aunt Hazel's bungalow."

"If you say so," the bird said agreeably.

"You must have—" Dodo stopped to listen. The bungalow had become quieter. The television was no longer on. She scrambled out of bed and began pushing the bird toward the window. "Quick. You can't stay here."

The bird pushed back. It was quite strong. "I've never been out there. I'm not going. It's too danger-ous. There are men with guns and cars that crash and—"

"You've been watching too much TV," Dodo said, unhooking the old-fashioned screen on the window. "The real world isn't like that. At least, not around here."

"Will I be back next week? Same time? Same channel?"

The floor in the dining room creaked. Dodo was prepared to say anything that would get the bird out before Aunt Hazel appeared.

"Sure. Up you go," she coaxed, shoving the bird from underneath. It was every bit as heavy as Arley. "Try to help."

Obligingly, the bird began to hop, allowing Dodo to raise it to the windowsill. It was standing there, gasping for breath, when Dodo heard Aunt Hazel begin to turn the knob to the door.

"Go on," she prodded. "Fly!"

After sending Dodo one last mournful look, the bird started flapping its wings. On the fifth flutter, it jumped.

"Ouch!"

The bird hadn't flown. It hadn't even glided. It had plummeted to the ground like a fifty-pound sack of potatoes.

CHAPTER 4

TAMARA

Arley and Aunt Hazel slept late. Rather than risk waking them, Dodo slipped into her seersucker shorts and a T-shirt and headed outdoors.

It was a beautiful morning, too early to be sticky hot, so quiet that Dodo could easily tell which bungalows were already stirring. From one came the soft clatter of dishes, from another the hum of a hair dryer. Except for a cat picking its way through a flower bed, she was alone in the lane. Overhead, gulls with wings outstretched flew toward the Sound. Dodo decided to follow their example. Sticking her arms out at her sides, she ran toward the wooden steps.

"Ee-eu! Ee-eu!" She imitated the gulls, tipping her arms from one side to the other.

On the fourth step from the bottom, she jumped, careful to avoid bumping an overturned rowboat, and landed hard on the pebbles that made up the beach. Ahead of her, the birds swooped gracefully to the water, where they bobbed up and down with the waves and eyed her with interest.

"You wouldn't believe the dream I had," she confided to them. "There was the weirdest bird."

"Are you talking to the gulls?"

At the question, Dodo turned back to the staircase. Tamara was poised halfway down, wearing sunglasses and a polka dot two-piece bathing suit. In her arms, she carried a towel and a bottle of lotion.

"Um, yes. I mean, no," Dodo stammered. "I think I was talking to you. Sort of."

"What do you mean, 'sort of'?"

Dodo searched her brain for something to say as Tamara finished descending the steps. "Are you going swimming?" she asked finally. Then, without allowing Tamara time to answer, she added, "Well, that's a stupid question. Of course you are."

"Why, are you?" Tamara asked.

"What?"

"Going swimming."

"Oh. Sure."

"In your shorts?"

Dodo smacked the side of her head, trying to look comical the way Barbie Fishbein might, only she used a little too much force and wound up smarting.

"Are you okay, Dorothy?"

"Yes. Of course."

For a while, neither girl spoke. Dodo's heart began to pound. This was her chance to make friends with Tamara, and she was wasting it. Say something interesting, she urged herself. "It's bigger today."

"What is?"

"The beach. See, the tide is out and more of the beach is uncovered."

"Oh. Yeah. I guess so." Looking uncomfortable, Tamara hesitated only a moment before turning around to walk back up the stairs.

"Have you forgotten something?" Dodo asked, rushing along behind her. She stopped short when a woman appeared by the seawall.

"Here we come. Sorry it took us so long, Tamara, honey. I had to finish packing the lunch. Who's this?"

Tamara looked momentarily blank. "Dorothy Penny."

"Dorothy Penny from school?"

As Tamara nodded, a man with a rubber dinghy balanced over his head came into view. To make way, everyone began walking down the steps to the beach.

"Fred," said the woman. "This is Dorothy Penny from back home. Isn't that nice? Now Tamara will have someone to play with."

Reaching the bottom of the staircase, the man raised and lowered the boat as if he were tipping a hat. "You're the girl we saw from the bungalow, aren't you?" he said. "The one who was dancing around and making noises?"

Dodo felt herself blush.

"Well, nice to meet you, Dorothy," Mr. Hughes called as he led his family across the beach. When he flipped the dinghy onto the water, the gulls that had been floating there took to the air, complaining at the disturbance. Touching down a short distance away, they watched warily as he helped his wife and daughter to step into the rubber boat.

"Say good-bye, Tamara," Mr. Hughes prompted, and Tamara fluttered her hand, filling Dodo with hope.

From now on, Dodo promised herself, she wouldn't do anything dumb like talk to gulls. And when she saw Tamara, she would say interesting things, so that Tamara would want to be friends.

Paddled one way by Mr. Hughes and pushed another by the gentle waves, the dinghy made slow progress. Rooted in place, Dodo stared after it until it drew alongside a sleek cabin cruiser, where all three of the Hugheses climbed aboard. With the rumble of an engine, the big boat came to life and headed out to deeper waters.

"Now what?" Dodo asked the birds, forgetting her recent resolve. "Tamara's gone. There's nothing to do."

With a sigh, she tried stretching out. Having no

towel or blanket, she had to keep shoving the pebbles about until she'd made a bed that molded to her frame. The sun had gotten stronger. Its rays beat down, reflecting off the water, seeming to treble both the light and the heat.

When she was as comfortable as she could get, Dodo closed her eyes and made a remarkable discovery: colors swam on the inside of her eyelids! First red fading to orange and yellow, and then green blending to blue. After a while, the colors formed themselves into shapes, as clouds might on a windy day. Relaxing more with every minute, Dodo studied the shifting patterns, and before long, she fell asleep.

———

"Are you going to waste the whole day?" Arley asked.

Dodo pretended she hadn't heard. She left her eyes closed, slowly becoming aware of sounds, of water lapping and boats humming and gulls crying.

"Aunt Hazel said have this for breakfast."

Shading her face with one hand, Dodo opened her eyes. Arley stood above her, holding out a raisin and nut granola bar.

"Also, she said don't go swimming alone."

Abruptly, Dodo sat up and slipped the package into her shorts pocket.

"Don't you say thanks?"

"Thanks," she replied absently. In the distance

she could see the outlines of some kind of barge. Closer in, but still far from shore, sailboats and speedboats moved. Tamara was out there.

Arley dug the toe of one sneaker into the beach. "You've been asleep forever. I've been watching you. Did you know that when your head's tilted back, you look just like a pig?" Without waiting for a reaction, he went on. "I had bad dreams all night long. I don't think I'm going to be able to sleep here at Aunt Hazel's."

Dodo put three fingers up to feel the bulb of her nose. "It's not being here that gave you bad dreams. It was the orange juice."

"You didn't have bad dreams?"

"Not bad dreams, exactly. More weird." Satisfied that her nose was in its usual shape, Dodo began sifting through the pebbles, shells, and dried seaweed that comprised the beach's surface. She picked up a flat rock and sent it skimming over the water. *Skip. Skip. Plop.* "Beat that!" she challenged.

Arley picked up a handful of stones. He flung them, all at once, onto the water. "Mine skipped a hundred times!" he bragged. "So what did you dream about?"

"Well, I dreamed that a bird—a huge, talking bird—had been living here in Aunt Hazel's bungalow. It seemed so real. I remember I made the bird jump out the window before Aunt Hazel came to bed."

"Did it say 'ouch' and make a thud when it landed?" Arley asked. "Like—"

"Like a Thanksgiving turkey hitting the floor," Dodo finished.

"I heard that," Arley said excitedly. "What time did you dream that Aunt Hazel went to bed?"

"A bit after twelve."

"That *is* when she went to bed," he said, turning to look at her. "Maybe you were awake."

Dodo shook her head. "Don't be silly."

"What about the feathers that were all around? I don't know if you noticed, but they weren't the same color as Aunt Hazel's stuffed pheasant. I'll bet they came from your talking bird."

"But the policemen searched the whole bungalow," Dodo reminded him. "If anything had been there, they would have found it."

"They were looking for a person. They wouldn't have noticed a bird. I mean, Aunt Hazel keeps lots of strange things from her trips."

As two gulls circled lazily overhead, Dodo thought about the punctured cans and the shape of the dream bird's beak. She thought about the ripped pillow that looked like a nest, and the egg Aunt Hazel had kept on top of the television, the egg that had been broken.

"Forget it," she said out loud, to herself as well as Arley. It had been bad enough when the Big Three caught her saving worms. It would be the end if

Tamara suspected she was capable of believing in a talking bird, one that had been hatched in her aunt's bungalow.

"Do you have a better explanation?" Arley asked.

"If what I dreamed wasn't a dream," Dodo reasoned, "where is the bird? A bird like that couldn't be hidden very easily. It would stick out. Somebody would hear it talk."

Arley began walking around. "I don't know. Maybe it's behind a bush now, or on a porch. Maybe it's under this rowboat."

He crouched down beside the boat at the bottom of the staircase. It sat on four cinder blocks. "Come here, Dodo," he called, struggling to lift the boat's side. "Help me."

Hoping Tamara didn't have a pair of binoculars on her cabin cruiser, Dodo went over to her brother. "I don't know why I'm doing this," she grumbled as she took hold of the boat on either side of an oarlock and tugged. "There isn't—"

She raised the boat a few inches.

"—any—"

With Arley's help, the boat moved up a few more inches.

"—talking—"

They could almost see the sand underneath it.
"—bird—"

"Hello," the bird said. "We'll be right back after these messages."

CHAPTER 5

━━━━▸

DIDUS
INEPTUS

Dodo and Arley both let go of the boat. It thudded onto the cinder blocks, sending up a puff of dust.

"Holy cow! What did it say?" Arley asked.

"I think it watched too much TV when it was in Aunt Hazel's bungalow," Dodo answered.

For two full minutes, they stood motionless, staring down in silence at the underside of the rowboat.

"It's big," Arley said finally.

"I told you it was."

"Excuse me." The bird's voice came hollowly. "Would you have any food?"

Dodo pulled the uneaten granola bar from her pocket.

"Well," her brother prodded. "Aren't you going to give it to the bird?"

Dodo's eyes wandered from the package in her palm to the blue horizon and then to the overturned boat. "No."

"What's the matter with you? Don't you see how

great this is? We could keep it and tame it and make it our pet!"

Dodo started walking toward the water. "I don't want to have anything to do with this."

"But the bird is hungry!" Arley said, stamping his foot on the stones.

"So feed it."

When Dodo tossed Arley the granola bar, he put his hands up to catch it. "I can't do it alone. You've got to help. Please, Dodo."

"You're not going to talk me into any more crazy schemes, Arley. Rescuing the worms was the last one."

"But it's not used to being outside," Arley pleaded as the bird made a noise like a sneeze. "If we don't help it, it might *die!*"

It was the same argument he had used for the worms. It had worked then, and, Dodo knew, it would work now. Despite what Tamara might think, Dodo couldn't bear to think of an animal suffering. Besides, Tamara was out somewhere on the water, probably for the whole day. There was no way she could know what Dodo was doing.

"All right," she said. "But if the bird makes one move to bite us, we call the animal shelter to come take it away."

Triumphant, Arley thrust the granola bar back into his sister's hand. "You crawl under the boat and feed the bird. I'll be right back."

"Where are you going?" Dodo asked. "Arley!"

But he had already run up the stairs and disappeared behind the seawall. Dodo sighed and got down to squeeze herself under the edge of the boat. "Stay where you are," she ordered nervously when she was halfway in. "Keep your distance!"

Although the area was dim, Dodo could see that the bird had not moved from its position under the stern of the boat. Sitting upright, she ripped open the foil paper and tossed its contents aft. The bird seemed to swallow it in one gulp.

"Got any Pattycake Cakes?" it asked.

"No."

"MacaroniOs?"

"No."

"Fruity-ade?"

"Sorry."

After a few moments, during which the bird pecked at the sand, searching for crumbs, Dodo asked, "Did you turn on Aunt Hazel's television?"

"Clever kids keep clear of electricity," the bird said gravely, parroting an ad Dodo had seen many times.

"So, as far as you know, it was on when you were hatched."

The bird nodded.

"What I figure," she said slowly, "is that some noise from outside turned on Aunt Hazel's television— That isn't too strange," she interrupted herself. "Sometimes, at home, when something makes just the right pitch, our old set goes on. It's hooked up to respond to the sound the remote makes. Anyhow, I'd guess that the television went on, and the heat or the radiation made you hatch."

"That's what I figure, too," the bird said.

Two thick books were thrust under the tent of the boat, followed quickly by Arley. "Is the creature still here?" he asked breathlessly.

Dodo knocked her head against the boat's seat. "Ow. Yes. You're crowding me. Find your own space."

For a few seconds, they shuttled about, getting comfortable. Neither of them wanted to be too close to the bird.

"Guess what?" Arley said excitedly, making himself a seat from one of the books. "I described what I could remember about the bird to Aunt Hazel, not saying that I'd seen it, of course, and she said it sounded like a dodo."

Dodo wrinkled her face. "A dodo?"

"Is that good?" asked the bird.

"I don't know," Arley answered. "I brought the D volume of the encyclopedia, though, and something else written by a guy named Darwin. Aunt Hazel said Darwin could explain what happened to the dodos."

Dodo thumbed through the pages of the encyclopedia. Because of the lack of light, she had to bend close to the pages to see the entries.

Dodge City.

Dodgson, Charles Lutwidge: *see* Carroll, Lewis.

Dodo.

" '*Didus ineptus*,' " she read. " 'Flightless bird of Mauritius. First seen by Portuguese sailors about 1507. Name derived from *doudo*, which is Portuguese for—' "

She stopped.

"For what?" Arley asked.

Pressing the tip of her finger over the word *silly*, she continued. " 'General appearance conveyed an air of stupidity.' "

The bird coughed gently.

" 'No natural enemies until the island was colonized. Settlers ate dodo meat; their dogs, cats and hogs ate dodo eggs—' "

She skimmed the rest of the paragraph, then looked up into the blinking eyes of the bird. "Pardon me, but you're extinct!"

The dodo shifted its weight and made a noise in its throat. "I could try using mouthwash. Two out of three dentists surveyed—"

"I didn't say *stink*, I said *extinct*," Dodo repeated. "It means you're not supposed to be alive. All the animals like you have been dead for—" She bent down close to the book again. "Since 1681. It says here, 'All that remains of the dodo are some skeletons, more or less complete, several heads, and a few feet.' "

"Aunt Hazel must have told me the wrong thing. If dodos are extinct, this bird can't be a dodo."

Dodo shoved the encyclopedia into Arley's lap so that he could study the picture. Faced with an image that exactly matched the bird under the boat, he conceded.

"Okay. It's a dodo, all right."

"Don't call it that," Dodo complained. "I don't want to hear that name anymore."

"So what should I call it?"

" 'Darwin' would be nice," the bird said.

"Where'd you get that?" Arley asked.

"You said it before. You said he knew what happened to the dodos."

Remembering the second book, Arley fished around in the shadows. "Where is that book?"

"You're sitting on it," Dodo told him. "Forget it for now. We have to figure out what we're going to do about . . . Darwin."

The dodo wriggled its tail feathers, pleased with the name.

"We're not calling the animal shelter," Arley said firmly. "Darwin has got to be pretty valuable, being extinct and all."

"Then I suppose we should take him to Aunt Hazel."

"She would—" Arley frowned, considering what Dodo had said. "You think Darwin is a boy?"

She studied the dodo. "Uh. Yes. It's a boy. A girl

wouldn't have such a stupid expression on her face."

Arley shook his head. "I'll bet it's a girl. Ask it."

"Asking wouldn't do any good. Watch." Dodo leaned toward the bird. "Do you think you might be a lion in disguise?"

Darwin glanced nervously from one to the other of them, sensing a test. Slowly, he began nodding his large head for yes. When he saw Arley's expression of disgust, he switched to no.

"She doesn't understand," Arley said. "Do you, Darwin, old girl? You are a girl, aren't you?"

"Yes," the bird said.

"You are a boy, aren't you?" Dodo asked quickly.

"Yes," the bird said again.

"You can't be both," Dodo scolded. "Do you lay eggs?"

"What are eggs?"

"There," Dodo said triumphantly, taking the bird's ignorance for a no. "Darwin doesn't know what eggs are, and there was no evidence of any having been laid in the bungalow. He's a boy. What are we going to do with him?"

"I don't think we should take him to Aunt Hazel," Arley said. "She'd only put him in a museum. Or the zoo."

"That's true." Recalling the sad eyes of the caged zoo animals and the fact that animals in museums were dead, Dodo shivered.

"Do they feed you in museums?" Darwin asked. "If Aunt Hazel puts me in a museum, will they feed me?"

"The poor guy's hungry!"

Realizing when Arley spoke how empty her own stomach was, Dodo said, "It must be about noon by now. The last thing we need is to have Aunt Hazel out searching for us. You stay here, Darwin. Arley and I will have our lunch and bring something back for you."

"Don't leave here," Arley warned the bird, ducking to follow his sister into the daylight. "No food if you do!"

The sun was directly overhead. Shielding her eyes against the sudden brightness, Dodo stared at the beach, where there were nearly a dozen people, both on the sand and in the water.

"All those people used the steps," she told Arley. "They passed right by us."

"Do you think they heard us talking to Darwin?"

"Probably. With luck, they thought we were playing. From now on, we'll have to be more careful."

Casting a last nervous glance back at the overturned rowboat, they started up the staircase, Arley with a book under each arm. When they reached the bungalow, they found Aunt Hazel rooting through the clutter on the porch. She had removed all the plastic from over the screens, and a slight breeze, scented by the sea, was ruffling her hair.

"Ah, here it is!" she exclaimed, holding up a battered white box.

"What is it?" Arley wanted to know.

"A cooler. First we'll shop, and then we're going to picnic on the beach!"

CHAPTER 6

SURVIVAL
OF
THE FITTEST

Dodo stared down at her own feet, which looked sort of green and very far away in the waist-high water. To and fro. To and fro. The water rocked gently, rhythmically. She lifted one foot, then lowered it again, clouding the bottom with a miniature sandstorm.

"How will I know if I'm going to step on a crab?" she asked nervously.

"You could watch your feet, which wouldn't be much fun, or you could swim without ever touching down, or you could stand still, which is what I want you to do right now," said Aunt Hazel.

Imagining an army of crabs patrolling the Sound's floor, Dodo waited impatiently for the water to clear. It hadn't taken her long to realize they would not be able to sneak any food to Darwin. After the trip to the grocery store and lunch, Aunt Hazel had set about introducing them to the beach.

"There!" Arley whispered excitedly. "See them? They're swimming in a school, just like you said they would, Aunt Hazel. Oh! They're going to swim right through our legs!"

Dodo held herself stiffly. She knew she shouldn't have come into the water with Arley and Aunt Hazel. She didn't want to see the fish. She didn't want their scaly bodies to touch her legs.

"There are hundreds of them!" Arley announced.

At first Dodo didn't see them, not until, seemingly with one mind, they shifted course. Suddenly their thin silver forms shimmered with sunlight, dispelling Dodo's fear.

"They're beautiful!" she exclaimed. When she lowered a hand into the water, hoping to touch one of the fish, the school darted away.

Beside her, Aunt Hazel reached up to adjust the straw hat she wore. "Lunch ought to be digested by now. Time for swimming tests."

"But we know how to swim," Arley boasted. "We took lessons at the Y."

"Then you'll pass my test," his aunt answered. "If you expect to roam about this summer, you'll first have to prove to me that you can take care of yourselves."

They were to get from shore to one of the moored boats and back again, taking however long they needed. Arley went first. Watching his arms churn the water, Aunt Hazel said, "He'll have to slow down. Looking for endurance, not speed."

Nearby, a red-shower-capped lady was stumbling

from the water. Dodo heard her mumble, "I hate these pebbles."

"How are you, Rose?" Aunt Hazel asked, nodding in a perfunctory way. "How's your mother this year?"

"Same as ever. I see you have little visitors with you."

"This is my niece, Dodo, and the boy swimming out there is my nephew, Arley."

"Howdy do," said Rose.

"Hello, Mrs.—"

"It's Miss Milton, but you can call me Rose. Everybody does."

"It's nice to meet you, Rose," Dodo said politely.

"I hate these pebbles," Rose repeated. Dodo watched her pick her way across the beach to the steps, carrying her bulk as if she were walking over broken glass.

"According to Darwin's theories," Aunt Hazel informed Dodo, "if we had to go about barefoot on ground such as this, our descendants would develop tougher soles."

"Darwin!" Did Aunt Hazel know about Darwin? Dodo tried to read her aunt's face, but Aunt Hazel's eyes were trained on Arley and told nothing. "Oh, *that* Darwin," Dodo said, realizing her aunt was not speaking about the dodo but about the man who had written the book Arley had brought under the boat. "Would they really?"

"He called it natural selection, or survival of the fittest."

"And he wrote about the dodo?"

"Indirectly. He said that what we don't use, we lose. For instance, the ability to fly."

Dodo was astounded. "We used to be able to fly?"

"Not us. The dodos. Because they had a very idyllic existence on their island—plenty of food and no predators—they grew fat and docile. Their wings became useless appendages. They left their eggs unprotected on the floor of the forest. When their environment changed—"

"They died out," Dodo finished.

Aunt Hazel nodded. "Precisely. They could not fly or run away from their enemies; they could not protect their eggs."

Arley had been taking a break from his swim, floating on his back about halfway between the moored boat and the beach. Dodo saw him start to swim again. When he staggered onto shore, he was breathless. "Do I pass?" he gasped.

"You do, indeed," Aunt Hazel said. "Next."

Reluctantly, Dodo stepped a few feet out, to where the bottom was sandy.

"You can do it," Arley called encouragingly as she splashed some water onto her arms and face. "It's not too hard if you don't rush."

With a quick dive forward, Dodo started swimming with slow, even strokes. One, she turned her face to the side. Two, she dipped it into the water. To the side. Back into the water.

Survival of the fittest, she thought. If only the dodos had been smart enough to change themselves.

One. Two. One. Two. Dodo stopped to tread water. She'd shifted off course a little to the left. Correcting her direction, she plunged ahead. One. Two. One. Two. Her arms sliced the water. Her legs kicked.

Arley was right, she told herself. Judging by Aunt Hazel's information, if they did not help the dodo, he would die. But how long could they help him before someone found out? And what would become of a talking bird when that happened?

One. Two. One. Two.

First, they had to get Darwin away from the bungalows, she decided as she reached the moored boat. He had to be hidden someplace safe where they could help him without letting anyone else see. Next, he had to change. And since he wasn't smart enough to change himself, she and Arley would have to do it for him.

Still thinking, Dodo set off for shore using the backstroke, never stopping until her arm butted the sandy bottom of the shallow water.

"Very good, Dodo," Aunt Hazel proclaimed.

"Are there any private places around here?" Dodo

demanded when she was on her feet again. "Places where nobody would see you? I mean, if you wanted to live outdoors and—"

"If you were a bird," Arley said, catching on.

Dodo glared at her brother. "Or *any* kind of animal."

Aunt Hazel thought for a moment. "There's the land bordering the bay. It's been set aside as a preserve for wildlife."

"How do we get there?" Arley asked.

Dodo glowered at him. "Shut up," she mouthed silently. Aunt Hazel didn't notice because she had bent down to pick up a stick and was tracing in the sand. The thing she drew looked like a witch's long, crooked finger.

"We're on a peninsula," she told them. "That's a bit of land surrounded on three sides by water. Over here we have the Sound and on the other side we have the bay."

"Where would the road be?" Dodo asked.

Aunt Hazel dragged the stick lengthwise through the drawing. "Right down the middle."

"That makes the preserve you were talking about across the street from here," Dodo said after she'd studied the crude map.

"Yes. That's why there are no buildings there—at least, none after the restaurants and arcades. People decided the wetlands needed protecting."

"Perfect!" Arley shouted.

Aunt Hazel straightened. "What's perfect?"

"Arley has these fits when he doesn't make any sense," Dodo said quickly. "It's nothing to worry about."

Arley was undampened. "Are we allowed to go to that land across the street? We proved that we can swim and take care of ourselves, so can we? Please?"

Dodo closed her eyes. Arley was probably ruining everything! *Why are you so anxious to go there?* Aunt Hazel would ask. *What are you hiding? Have you found some rare kind of bird?*

Hearing no answer to Arley's question other than the quiet shush of the waves, Dodo opened her eyes. Aunt Hazel didn't look suspicious, Dodo thought. But maybe she would forbid them to set foot on the protected land. *It's against the law to go there,* she might say.

"I was thinking about setting a goal for the two of you," Aunt Hazel said at last. "Just because it's summer is no reason to let your minds go soft. I'd like you to work on a project. You know, gather shells or insects or plants and categorize what you find."

"So may we go across the street?" Arley persisted.

"Yes, indeed. It will be a very good place to find specimens. But you mustn't disturb the wildlife."

Arley grinned smugly at his sister as Aunt Hazel shook out their towels.

"I've got everything you'll need back at the bungalow," Aunt Hazel went on enthusiastically. "Dodo, pack up that cooler. Arley, fold up my chair. We'll use the rest of today to get you set up."

Arley's smirk evaporated as he and Dodo exchanged anxious glances. Would the hungry bird stay in its hiding place until one of them could sneak it food?

⊷⊶

Back in the bungalow, there wasn't much time to think about Darwin. When Aunt Hazel wasn't laying out tweezers and brushes and guidebooks, she was reciting tales of her adventures. Every so often, she would stop to interject, "Decided on a project yet?"

Dodo eventually chose bird watching since it was an activity that called for a minimum of equipment. Arley, fascinated by the assortment of specimen bottles and labels, agreed to collect something, although he couldn't settle on what that something would be.

By dinnertime, the children were exchanging abbreviated plans whenever Aunt Hazel was out of hearing range.

"Darwin after bedtime!"

"Leftover chicken!"

Horrified, Dodo forgot about whispering. "That would practically make him a cannibal!"

"What's that?" Aunt Hazel asked as she emerged from the tiny kitchen with a platter of broiled chicken balanced in one hand and a plate of potatoes in the other. "Can of what?"

Dodo swallowed hard. "Uh. Can—can-able. We were wondering if chicken was can-able."

Aunt Hazel set the dinner on the table. "Are you asking if one can put chicken in a can? I suppose so, but with me cooking, you'd better worry about whether it's edible, not can-able."

While Aunt Hazel laughed at her own joke, Dodo rolled her eyes and sighed. Something told her it wasn't going to be easy keeping Darwin a secret.

<hr />

Although Dodo did her best to stay awake, the day's combination of sun and salt water conspired against her. It was past midnight when she woke and remembered their plans. Aunt Hazel lay beside her, her breathing shallow and regular. Moving carefully, Dodo slipped out of bed and into the dining room. The first thing she noticed was that the TV was on in the living room. The next was that there were *two* figures sitting on the couch.

Dodo quickly pulled herself back into the safe darkness of the bedroom doorway. One of the people was Arley. She'd recognized his cowlick. But who was the other?

Cautiously, she leaned forward. Then, placing each foot carefully on the floor so that the wood didn't creak, she inched toward the couch.

"Just what do you think you're doing?" she hissed when she was close enough to see.

"Shh," said Darwin. "I want to watch the commercial for Super-Pest-Be-Gone. In case we ever have a problem with rats or bugs. It's not available in stores, you know."

"You can't stay here," Dodo told him, reaching out to shut off the television, which was playing with the sound very low. "Aunt Hazel will see you. She'll want to stick you in a specimen bottle and put a label on you and conduct experiments to figure out why you exist—"

"And feed me?"

Arley picked up a bag of Corny Chips from the side of the couch. He held it open for Darwin. "We'll feed you. We won't let anything bad happen to you."

"We won't have control over what happens to him if he stays around here," Dodo insisted. "You shouldn't have brought him in, Arley."

"I didn't. He showed up all by himself."

Having finished the chips in the bag, Darwin waddled over to the television to study the control knobs. "Which one turns it back on?"

Obligingly, Arley pulled on the proper knob. As an animated mouse raced across the screen, he asked Dodo, "Did you know that channel fifty shows old cartoons at night?"

" *'Fifty's the one to watch!'* " Darwin sang. The last word of the jingle was cut short as Arley snapped the bird's bill closed with his hands.

Dodo picked up a flattened cookie wrapper and a container of macaroni salad, which was nearly empty. She shook them at her brother. "He shouldn't be eating this junk. Survival of the fittest!"

Releasing Darwin, Arley held a finger to his lips to remind Dodo to keep quiet. "What are you talking about?"

"Darwin has got to change, and you and I are going to change him."

Arley resettled himself on the couch and studied Darwin. Standing in front of the television, the bird was completely absorbed in the cartoon. "Why does he have to change?"

"In order to survive. I know you think it would be fun to keep Darwin as a pet, but you know it wouldn't really work. At the end of the summer, we'll go home, and Darwin will be left to take care of himself."

"Look," Darwin said. "The mouse is going to run into that doghouse."

Arley nodded at Dodo, half his attention focused

on the sight of a cat rushing headlong after the mouse. "I suppose you're right. He'll have to know how to use the stove and how to turn on the TV and how to run the vacuum so that when he stays in the bungalow again, he won't make it a wreck."

Dodo snapped off the set just as the cartoon dog woke up. "No. Darwin has got to be able to survive out in the wild."

"Wild?" Darwin repeated, looking slightly nervous.

"Every day, we'll go to him and teach him what he needs to know," Dodo went on. "Like what to eat. He's simply got to lose weight. And he's got to strengthen his wings with exercise."

Arley looked over at the bird. "I like him the way he is."

"Don't forget what happened to all the other dodos."

Darwin nodded his big head knowingly. "They stunk."

Arley muffled his laughter with one hand. "You know, they probably did!"

"What you mean to say," Dodo began patiently, "is that they became—"

"Stinky," Darwin finished.

"No, *extinct.*"

"Oh."

Arley checked the Corny Chips bag for crumbs before he faced the bird. "I hate to say it, but Dodo might be right, Darwin. I guess you can't stay here."

"But I like it here."

"It's too dangerous."

"Men with guns?"

"Yes. That's it."

Dodo bristled at the lie. "Arley!"

"Well, something has to make him stay where we put him," Arley said defensively. He turned back to the bird. "We're going to send you to a hideout so you'll be safe from guns and stuff."

Darwin's tail wagged. "That sounds like fun. Do I need a disguise?"

Arley shook his head. "No, but you have to move out now while it's dark so that no one sees you."

"We'll come first thing in the morning," Dodo promised.

"Did you ever see *The Guns of Rattlesnake Creek*?" Darwin asked as they steered him onto the porch. "This is just like the time Gerard Vabulous had to sneak past the bunkhouse without waking up the cowhands. Okay, pardner. Just point my horse in the right direction."

CHAPTER 7

━━━━━►

THE
BRILLIANT
DOROTHY PENNY

Early the next morning, Dodo started up the lane with a narrow guidebook in her shirt pocket and a small pair of binoculars bouncing from a strap around her neck. Her thoughts were full of Darwin.

"Dodo, Aunt Hazel packed us lunch!" Arley shouted as he catapulted from the bungalow after her.

"What did he call you?"

Tamara seemed to appear from nowhere. Startled, Dodo put on as innocent a face as she could manage. "What did who call me?"

"Your brother."

"Oh. Um. He's called Arley."

"I know that, Dorothy. I asked what he called *you*."

"Why, Dorothy, of course. What else would he call me? Anything else would be—"

Arley's voice interrupted her. "What do you think, Dodo? She even put in two Pattycake Cakes!"

Dodo stood mute as Arley came skidding to a halt beside her.

"He called you Dodo," Tamara said. "Why did he call you Dodo? Is that your nickname? I thought a dodo was some kind of stupid bird—"

Dodo didn't wait to hear any more. She took off, leaving Arley chasing after her. Up the lane, across the road in front of the big house, into a dense wood, and then down to the bay shore.

"Wait up!" Arley pleaded as he struggled down a slope thick with weeds and wild roses. "Ouch! Dodo, wait up!"

Meeting mud, Dodo stopped and looked out at the reeds edging the bay. As a light breeze passed over them, they swayed and waved like a great green sea.

"I'm sorry," Arley panted when he reached her side. He dropped his backpack down onto the damp ground of the preserve. "Honestly. I didn't see her. What's wrong with being called Dodo, anyway? It's a good name."

"Yeah, for a stupid bird."

"No, for you. I like it better than Dorothy."

Dodo punched her brother in the arm. Then, feeling better, she asked, "Where do you suppose Darwin is?"

"We told him not to stop until he came to water," Arley said, rubbing his arm gingerly. "He's got to be around here somewhere. Let's look for tracks."

They began walking eastward, along a thin strip

of coarse sand that separated the incline from the mud and vegetation of the wetlands. The woods of the preserve were about nine feet above them.

Aunt Hazel had been right when she'd said this spot was private, Dodo thought, breathing in the heavy salt air. Civilization could have been a hundred miles away rather than the hundred yards it was in reality. The idea gave Dodo a feeling of peace, which was quickly shattered when Arley latched on to her arm.

"Hold it," he said in a hushed tone. "I think I heard something move."

After shaking him off, Dodo stopped and listened. The only sound was the pulsing whine of a speedboat bouncing across the bay. Thinking that Arley was imagining things, she started forward again, only to be grabbed once more.

"Hear it?"

She nodded. "I heard something that time. Soft. Like a whisper."

When Dodo bent to get closer to the source of the sound, the ground came alive.

"Crabs!" Arley announced with delight.

Scattered about in the mud at the base of the reeds were small circular holes, some inhabited, some not. With each of the children's movements, a platoon of crabs scurried toward cover.

"I think they're fiddler crabs," Arley said, trying to coax one from its mud cave. The creature was braver than most of its neighbors. As Arley put out a finger, it sidled forward with its larger claw ready for battle.

"Leave it alone," Dodo ordered. "We're looking for Darwin, remember? Let's keep moving."

Reluctantly, Arley stood up and followed his sister along the beach. They had arrived at low tide. In some of the places they walked, the water was as far away as the distant boats where men stood raking the bottom of the bay for clams and oysters. Other times, without warning, they came upon an inlet or tidal pool made secret by the reeds. In one inlet, they surprised a large, white wading bird.

"I dub this Lake Flapperfoot," Arley declared, watching the feet of the bird dangle as it tucked back its head and took to the air. He had decided that, as explorers, they were entitled to name any interesting landmark they came to. Behind them already were Hamburger Rock and Arley River.

"I'd call it Lake Mosquito," a voice said from somewhere nearby.

"Lake Flapperfoot," Arley insisted.

"But the flapperfoot leaves and the mosquitoes won't."

Dodo looked around for Darwin. Seeing him crouched inside a drainage pipe that protruded from the slope, she cried, "There he is!"

"What did you bring me?" the bird asked.

Before Arley could answer, Dodo stepped between

him and the bird. "We didn't bring you anything. That is, nothing but the answers to all your problems."

"My problem is that I'm hungry," the bird said.

With a little flourish, Dodo pulled a pad from her shorts pocket. "And we're going to teach you what to eat. That will be Lesson Number One. We'll make a list of every food you can find around here, then we'll break for calisthenics."

"What do they taste like?"

"You don't eat calisthenics, Darwin. You do them. They're exercises."

"Oh."

Dodo began to pace the area, her eyes alert. "Come on, Arley. Help. What do the wild birds eat?"

"Some eat fish."

Dodo made a notation on her pad. "Right."

"Excuse me. How would I get a fish?" Darwin asked. "And aren't all the fish around here still alive? Wouldn't it be simpler just to open a can?"

Dodo didn't answer. She was too busy writing. "Berries. Bugs. Worms. Hey, I'll bet some of the water birds eat crabs. Probably clams, too."

As Darwin plumped onto a thatch of dried reeds, Arley wandered up the slope and into the trees. He came back to the bird with his hands cupped together. "I found a mulberry tree," he announced.

Hesitantly, Darwin sampled one of the purplish

black fruits. Once it was gone, he looked for more.

"Try this," Dodo suggested, holding out a tuft of grass.

"Blech!"

Arley shook his head. "You think he's a cow or something, Dodo?"

"Well, I don't know what dodos eat."

"They don't eat *that,*" Darwin said.

"All right, then. Try a crab."

At Dodo's insistence, Darwin stood at the water's edge, motionless, his black beak close to the mud.

"Now!" she shouted when one of the larger crabs came within range.

Instantly, Darwin's head popped up, the crab with it. Unfortunately, the crab had been quicker than the bird. It had attached its claw firmly to the red sheath that covered the hooked tip of Darwin's bill.

"Get it off!" Darwin cried, attempting to shake the creature loose.

Arley tried to help. "Ow. Hey, watch it!" he yelled.

Several of his fingers were pinched before he could lower the crab to the marsh. There, it opened and closed its claw, boasting of victory. Feeling guilty, Dodo went off and gathered as many mulberries as Darwin could eat.

"There's still a lot of room in my stomach," the bird admitted when she'd made three trips, "but it's not mulberry room. It's Pattycake Cakes room."

"You shouldn't be too full when you exercise, anyway," Dodo told him. "Okay. Hold your wings up and stretch."

The bird didn't turn out to be very good at following directions. When he was supposed to circle his head, he circled his eyes. When he tried to lift one foot, he fell over.

"We'll jog," Dodo said with determination. "Anybody can jog. That will build up your endurance and help you to lose that flab. Ready? Follow me."

Shortening her steps so that the bird could keep up, Dodo set off down the beach. Darwin followed for about ten paces, then collapsed in an exhausted heap.

"Can we . . . can we . . . change the channel?"

Instead of answering, Dodo went directly to Hamburger Rock, where Arley sat laughing. One shove sent him off its side. He rolled about in hysterics, holding his stomach.

"Give it up, Dodo. You have about as much of a chance of changing Darwin as as you do turning yourself into a dodo bird!"

Dodo's whole body stiffened as an idea occurred to her. "That's it! That's it!"

Realizing he had been lying in mud, Arley sobered. "What's it? You want to be a dodo bird?"

"Ha-ha-ha! Ha-*hee*-ha!"

"Are you going nuts?"

Dodo was smiling a huge smile. "I'm a genius, Arley. You see before you the brilliant Dorothy Penny, girl genius!"

"You don't have to go nuts, Dodo," Arley muttered, turning his attention to his blackened legs and clothes. "You *are* nuts."

Dodo was oblivious to the insult. She wrapped her arms around herself and squeezed tight. She had had a brilliant idea: while she was changing Darwin, she would change herself, as well! She would become like Barbie Fishbein and Gigi Bell. She would copy their expressions and their phrases, becoming so much like them that Tamara would just have to like her!

"Ha-ha-ha-*hee*-ha!" she crowed. "Ha-ha-ha-*hee*-ha!"

Recovered from his exertion, Darwin got to his feet and ambled to Dodo's side. "Are you choking?"

"No. That's the way this girl, Barbie, laughs. Sort of. I haven't got it down just right. The last part should be higher, I think. Ha-ha-ha-*heeee*-ha!"

Darwin warmed up his voice with the Pattycake Cakes song, then executed the laugh. "Like that?"

"Yes! Exactly like that!" Dodo said, clapping her hands excitedly. "Do it again."

Completely disgusted with the proceedings, Arley sat down again on the large, flat-topped rock. He unzipped the backpack and took out his canteen, which Aunt Hazel had filled with apple juice.

"We'll practice laughing for fifteen minutes or so, then we'll jog some more," Dodo was saying. "How's this? Ha-ha-ha-HEEE-ha!"

⊷⊶

When the tide was about halfway in to shore, Dodo and Arley left Darwin hidden in the drainage pipe and started back to the lane. They found Aunt Hazel on a lawn chair in front of the bungalow.

"How did everything go?" she asked, setting the book she had been reading in her lap.

"Great," Arley answered. "I've decided to collect sea glass."

Aunt Hazel peered over the top of her sunglasses to the smooth piece of green lying on Arley's palm.

"I tried to tell him it was a dumb idea," Dodo interjected, "that he was collecting garbage, but would he listen to me? No!"

Arley picked up the glass and held it to the light. "This is my first specimen. I figure it came from a beer bottle. Probably imported."

Dutifully, Dodo opened her pad to the page after Darwin's diet. "I saw five swans and two geese, possibly brant, three crows, a heron, lots of sparrows, and a redwing blackbird."

"Not to mention a dodo," Arley said under his breath, earning a jab from his sister's elbow.

Aunt Hazel rubbed her eyes. "Um, that's fine. You've certainly earned a good dinner. What do you say we visit Davy Jones's Locker? I hear they've having a special on crabs."

Arley exhaled slowly. His fingers had begun throbbing. "Would I be able to get something else? Like a cheeseburger?"

"Done," Aunt Hazel said, slapping her book shut. "That is, provided you take a shower."

"Done," Arley agreed.

CHAPTER 8

THE
NATURALIST'S
DIARY

MONDAY:
sea gulls ~~||||~~ ~~||||~~ ~~||||~~ ||
redwing blackbirds ||
crows |||
sparrows ~~||||~~ ||

TUESDAY:
gulls—heaps
sparrows—ditto
swans ~~||||~~ (*a family of mother, father*
                     & 3 babies)
crows ||||
blue jay |

WEDNESDAY:
gulls—at least two dozen
starlings ~~||||~~ ||||
cardinals ||
mockingbird |

THURSDAY:
Everything like Tuesday plus one crane with black legs and yellow feet which I can't find in the guidebook.

FRIDAY:
Aunt Hazel doesn't want to see my notebook. I asked her yesterday, and she said she wasn't my teacher, and that one of the points of the project is to show that learning is fun. (Arley said, "Sure it is," like he didn't believe her at all.) Aunt Hazel says I should make notes, not keep score. She told me that Darwin—the writer guy, not the dodo—kept notes on his beagle or something. Sounds pretty boring to me.

Anyway, today I saw a bunch of gulls, like always. (My book says there are 50 different species!) I think they're neat because they hardly work at all when they're flying. They just hold out their wings and glide on the air currents. Not like the swans, who work hard just to get a few feet up off the water. Swans must flap their wings a hundred times a minute when they take off. When they come down again, they seem glad to be swimming.

I saw Tamara this morning. She was on her way to the beach. I guess she was going out on her boat again. She said "Hi" but didn't smile.

SATURDAY:

Tamara hates me. I know it. This morning, when I was waiting for Arley to finish breakfast, I saw her sitting on the steps to her bungalow, and I went over. She had a magazine. At first I acted like I was interested in the pictures, but pretty soon I got to looking at her skin. It's perfect. She doesn't have even one freckle! I wear sunscreen to keep from getting burned, but still the freckles come out. I must have a zillion. When Tamara caught me staring at her, she gave me a weird look and went inside, pretending that she had to help her mother. She hates me. Well, maybe she doesn't hate me, but she doesn't care that I'm alive.

Today, we saw a big, white bird with a long neck and a straight, pointy beak standing in some shallow water, surrounded by marsh grass. It stayed so perfectly still that Arley was sure it was fake, made out of cardboard or something. To prove him wrong, I started looking for a picture of it in the guidebook. To prove me wrong, Arley took off his sneakers and starting wading out into the bay. All of a sudden, the bird flew up, startling Arley so much that he fell into the water. He looked really funny, wet from the waist down. Best of all, since I won the bet, he had to take my turn at drying the dishes! (I think the bird was an American egret.)

MONDAY:

Darwin can jog longer now, and he looks a little thinner to me, though, with his feathers, it's hard to tell. I wonder what he'll eat when the mulberries are gone.

Today, in a tree that was half dead, I saw a woodpecker! It had a red head and was pecking away, just like woodpeckers always do in cartoons. This one didn't make a hole, though. Arley said it was eating bugs. I think he was right.

TUESDAY:

Jogging today, each time I turned my head to check on Darwin, he was farther and farther behind me—even though I kept adjusting my pace to match his. When I reached the spot where we always turn around, Darwin hadn't even made it halfway up the beach! Darwin swore he was trying, but I think he must be playing some kind of game with me—jogging only when I turn around. A kind of reverse "Red Light, Green Light, One Two Three."

Didn't see Tamara at all today.

WEDNESDAY:

Poor Darwin! I feel so bad for thinking he wasn't trying to get into shape. Today, when we were running, he cut his foot on the lid of a can! I tried to rip off the bottom of my shirt to make a tourni-

quet, the way they always do in the movies, but the stupid shirt wouldn't rip. Fortunately, when Arley held Darwin's foot in the water to wash off the wound, the bleeding stopped pretty quickly. I was glad because I had been all set to run and get Aunt Hazel. And if I'd had to spoil Darwin's secret, he would have been in another kind of danger. (I wonder where the can came from.)

FRIDAY:
Even though it was a rainy sort of day—overcast, mist alternating with drizzle—Arley and I went to the bay beach just the same. (Aunt Hazel said we may go out in any weather except thunderstorms.) The one time it began to rain hard, we saw two herons fly up out of the marsh. (Aunt Hazel said that the smaller birds we see are probably not American egrets but little blue herons, young ones. They start out white.) It was the first time any of them had ever flown over our heads, and we wondered where they were going. So we scrambled up the slope by the drainage pipe just in time to see them land in a maple tree! I didn't know they could do that. They're simply huge compared to other birds, like robins and starlings. They looked so funny perched in a tree, with their long, long legs. Darwin said he'd like to know what it was like, being in a tree, and Arley asked him how he was ever going to get up there to find out. I could see

that Darwin felt sad, so I said he might find out if he kept up my exercise program. Lately I'm working at strengthening his wings by moving them back and forth. I hope it helps. Since it's no effort, Darwin doesn't mind. Sometimes, when I'm doing it, he and Arley ignore me completely and talk about some stupid soap opera Darwin got used to watching when he was living in Aunt Hazel's bungalow.

The herons stayed in the maple until the rain let up, then they flew out toward the water again. It was exciting to see them. I wonder if Tamara would have thought so.

SATURDAY:
I found the name for that black-legged, yellow-footed crane. It turns out it's not a crane at all. It's a snowy egret. (Cranes fly with their necks long and their heads stuck out in front. Herons and egrets tuck their heads back by their shoulders when they fly, bending their necks into a kind of S shape.)

MONDAY:
Tamara met us in the lane this morning. She asked me where we were going. I got all flustered. Arley grabbed my arm and said, "For a walk." How rude! I wish I'd thought of something better to tell her.

We saw the weirdest bird today. Almost as weird

as Darwin. In fact, Arley thought we'd found another dodo—a baby one! It was fat like Darwin and the same slate gray color. I think it was a coot. But there were two major differences between this bird and Darwin. (1) Darwin is much bigger; and (2) The coot's bill is mostly white with red spots, while Darwin's is mostly black with a red tip. Even though both birds are strange looking, as I told Arley, I would never have confused them.

TUESDAY:
Darwin is definitely not getting thinner. We were playing with an old piece of Styrofoam that had washed in, pretending it was a pirate ship, and when I tried to lift Darwin aboard, I discovered that he's solid under those feathers! How can he stay fat on a diet of berries and bugs?

WEDNESDAY:
The Hugheses' boat motor needs fixing. They're not going out on the water for a couple of days. Tamara saw us on the Sound beach in the afternoon and said she'd come walking with us the next morning. Since we can't let her know about Darwin, I said something dumb about not being sure we would go for a walk. Tamara must have gotten the idea that I didn't want her around because she turned on her radio and didn't say anything more.

Tomorrow, I'll let Arley go to the bay by himself.

One day of no exercise shouldn't hurt Darwin too much. Then Tamara and I could take a real walk. Together!

THURSDAY:
I stayed around the lane for two hours this morning and never saw a sign of Tamara! Later on, I found out that she'd gone shopping with her mother.

CHAPTER 9

A DAY
ON
THE BAY

"How would you like to do something different to-day?" Aunt Hazel asked at breakfast on Friday.

Dodo was staring into a hand mirror, trying to unravel the mysteries of Gigi's smile. Why did the twist that made Gigi look full of fun make Dodo look as if she was smirking? Carefully, Dodo pulled back one side of her mouth. There. Now for the other. Just the tiniest bit higher, she told herself. As her top lip began to quiver, she let the smile fall. "Do something different like what?"

Aunt Hazel shrugged. "Whatever you please. Since we got here, you've spent nearly every morning in the preserve and every afternoon at our beach, swimming. Just thought you might need a change. Is there anything you'd especially like to do?"

Arley sat down and bit off a corner of toast. "I'd like to go to that video arcade. Play some Space Piloteer." He nibbled at the bread, shaping it into a gun, which he aimed at Dodo. *"P'shew, p'shew, p'shew.* Take that, you crummy meteor."

After trying in vain to picture Tamara steering down a bright green racetrack, animated cars spinning out of control around her, Dodo decided video games were not a Big Three thing. "Arcades give me a headache," she said, speaking to her mirror image.

"Then perhaps you could spend some time with the Hughes girl."

At Aunt Hazel's suggestion, Dodo nearly lost her grip on the mirror's handle. "Do you think I could? I mean, do you think she'd want to?"

"Only way to find out is to ask. And I see Mrs. Hughes right now. She must be heading for their boat."

After making one more attempt at Gigi's smile for good luck, Dodo flew to the porch door where she could see Aunt Hazel and Mrs. Hughes in the lane.

". . . Wondered . . . different type of day . . ."

Words, disconnected, reached her ears. She strained to hear what the women were saying.

". . . Of course . . . only too glad . . . Tamara . . . company."

Mrs. Hughes was agreeing! She was saying yes!

Realizing that she was wearing the bathing suit with the tired elastic, Dodo raced to the bedroom. By the time Aunt Hazel came back inside, she had changed into her best swimsuit and was grabbing a towel.

"Slow down," Aunt Hazel called. "Mr. Hughes will be taking Tamara and her mother out to the boat first. Wait while I get something for you to bring along."

"But I don't need anything!"

Ignoring Dodo's impatience, Aunt Hazel went to the kitchen to rummage in the cupboards. Dodo could hear her talking to herself. "Cookies? No. Somebody's opened them. Where's that box of Pattycake Cakes? Who's been in here? I can't find anything!"

"Do you think Darwin will be all right?"

Dodo threw her brother a distracted glance. "What? Oh, he'll be fine. I mean, he'll have to be by himself all winter. He might as well get used to it."

"I wish we could have told him our plans," Arley whispered."He'll be expecting us."

"Then don't go to the video arcade."

"Then you don't go with Tamara," Arley countered.

Aunt Hazel came out of the kitchen with a bag of pretzels. "Here you are, Dodo. It's all I could find. We'll have to go shopping again. We're out of everything."

<hr>

"Ha-ha-ha-*hee*-ha!" Dodo practiced nervously as she hurried for the staircase, hugging the pretzels to herself to keep them from bouncing about in the bag. "Ha-*hee*-ha-ha-*hee*-ha!" she laughed as she pattered down the steps to the beach. She could see Mr. Hughes waiting with the rubber dinghy. The small craft was lying on the water near shore, rocking with the waves.

"Do you know how to swim, Dorothy?" Mr. Hughes asked, pushing off and then sitting down on a sling seat opposite her.

Dodo's attention was on the cabin cruiser ahead of them. She nodded her answer, watching Tamara walk about on the big boat's deck.

"Good," Mr. Hughes said, dipping the oars into the water and then pulling. "Tamara's a pretty good swimmer, herself. That's important for boating."

Dodo nodded again. This is it, she thought. Tamara and Dorothy. Dorothy and Tamara. She hugged the bag of pretzels closer.

As he rowed, Mr. Hughes rambled on about fishing and tides, but Dodo only half listened. She was imagining her own face with Gigi's bright smile. She heard herself laughing with Barbie's laugh and saw herself fascinating Tamara with her every word.

"A pretzel, my dear?"

In reaching out to take what was offered, the imaginary Tamara blurred and became Arley. *"But what about Darwin?"*

With a pang, Dodo was brought back to reality. What *would* the bird think when neither she nor Arley arrived for the usual lessons? Would he be safe, as she had told Arley? Or would he do something dumb, like search for them?

It was hard to worry about Darwin, though, when Mrs. Hughes extended a hand over the side of the cabin cruiser. Scrambling aboard, Dodo pulled the corners of her mouth back and up.

"Hi, Tamara!" she said, feeling light-headed with excitement.

Tamara eyed Dodo curiously. When she motioned for Dodo to take a place on the bench seat that spanned the side of the boat, Dodo adjusted her lips nervously.

"What's the matter?" Tamara asked. "I can move over if you haven't got enough room."

Dodo smacked the side of her head, the way Barbie Fishbein would have. "Hey, I've got plenty of room!" she said. Then, trying Gigi's smile again, she pulled her lips up a bit more than back.

"Maybe you'd better loosen your life jacket," Tamara suggested. "You don't look so good."

"Oh, but I'm fine!" Dodo protested as Mr. Hughes started the inboard motor. "Where are we going?"

Tamara spoke up over the noise of the engine. "Around into the bay. My father has to do some paperwork for his job. He wants to moor someplace sheltered so he doesn't get seasick."

The boat rumbled eastward. Abandoning Gigi's smile for the moment, Dodo watched the shoreline change. After the bungalows and some weatherworn old houses came larger, newer homes. They were followed by a few public beaches, some stately old houses, and then some more bungalows. Finally there were mansions set on huge green tracts.

"That's the yacht club," Tamara said, indicating a large white building surrounded by tennis courts and elaborate shrubbery. "The village is over there, on the other side of the water."

Remembering the map Aunt Hazel had traced in the sand, Dodo knew they had reached the place where the peninsula curved around. The boat was entering the bay. After giving the group of buildings Tamara had pointed out a cursory glance, Dodo turned her gaze to the peninsula's shore, which was separated from them now by several miles of water.

"Everything looks so different from a boat," she said, nodding at the marshy coast.

"Have you been over there?"

"Yes. No. I don't know. Maybe." Dodo wasn't sure what she should answer. "What I mean is, Arley and I have taken walks, but I'm not sure where."

It was impossible to pick out landmarks from their position in the bay. Hamburger Rock, Lake Flapperfoot, and the drainage pipe were all hidden from sight by cattails and reeds and sea lavender.

And, Dodo told herself with relief, so was Darwin.

Mrs. Hughes had been riding below deck. As her husband threw out the anchor, she approached the girls with a magazine in hand. "Daddy's going to work, and I'm going to sit up here and read," she told her daughter. "I'll bet you two girls could have a great time taking out the dinghy. You could chatter away and not have to worry about bothering anyone."

Tamara said nothing, but the look on her face told Dodo she was not pleased about having to go out in the little rubber boat. Without Dodo along for the day, she would have been free to stay aboard, to listen to her radio or read. Now she was bound to entertain Dodo.

"I'll hand you the oars," she said, in what Dodo took to be a bored way. "Be careful to sit in the middle or you'll tip over."

After pulling the dinghy alongside, Dodo did as she was told. Then, wanting to ease the situation, she offered to do the rowing. It didn't take her long to discover that the chore was harder than it looked. Sometimes the oars dipped too deep and Dodo could hardly push at the water. Other times they barely skimmed the surface, and her energy was spent in wild jolts.

"Let me do it," Tamara said, taking over.

With Tamara working, it wasn't long before the craft was skirting the edge of the wetlands. Seemingly out of politeness, she pointed out to Dodo that the reeds did not grow uniformly, but in sections, one high, one a little lower, with channels cutting through them. Then, her duty apparently done, she left the boat to drift and leaned back to look at the sky.

The silence that ensued was unbearable to Dodo. She had to do something, she thought, or the day would be a disaster!

Just as Dodo opened her mouth to try Barbie's laugh, another laugh pealed across the water.

"Did you hear that?" Tamara asked, jerking herself into a seated position. The boat reacted with a series of little rolls.

"Ha-ha-ha-*hee*-ha!" Dodo exploded. She wanted Tamara to think the first burst of laughter had come from her, too, but Tamara wasn't fooled. Taking up the oars again, she began maneuvering the dinghy into the reeds.

"Be quiet, Dorothy. That's Barbie Fishbein. I'd know Barbie's laugh anywhere."

"It can't be Barbie," Dodo argued. "Let's turn around. Here. Let me row again."

With a silent shake of her head, Tamara moved them steadily toward shore.

The laughter continued. Desperate, Dodo twisted around and strained forward. With the tide high, they were going to be able to float all the way in! If only she could see Darwin first and warn him off, she thought. Tamara just *mustn't* find out about him! What would become of Darwin?

"Barbie?" Tamara called questioningly when one

of the laughs was cut dead. In its place came a growl. The growl intensified and was joined by others.

"Help!"

Hearing the weak voice, Tamara screamed, "We're coming! Hold on, Barbie!"

It was eerie gliding through the jungle of reeds to who knew what. As the sharp blades of grass began slapping at Dodo's arms and face, she reached over the front of the boat to make it move faster. The growls had turned into vicious snarls. Why was there no sound from Darwin? Were they too late?

When the dinghy burst into the clearing, Dodo saw Darwin surrounded by three large dogs. She leaped from the boat with her arms flailing.

"Go home! Scram! Get out of here, you mangy mutts!"

Hearing her words, one of the dogs tucked its tail between its legs and retreated. The other two, however, were undeterred. As Dodo watched, the bird disappeared beneath a blur of fur.

"Go for the water!" she cried, plunging after him.

Luckily, in their frenzy to get at Darwin, the dogs ignored Dodo. Feeling a collar around the neck of the black one, she grabbed and pulled, enabling the bird to flounder into the shallow water. Immediately, though, he was pursued by a larger, brown dog.

"Move away, Dorothy."

Dodo had forgotten she was not alone. Looking up, she saw Tamara above her with an oar in her hands.

"Move away," Tamara repeated. "You're going to get bitten."

Thwack!

The brown dog yelped and spun about as Tamara wielded the oar.

Thwack, thwack!

At first the dogs were too surprised to do anything. They backed away and stared at Tamara. Dodo stared, too. This wasn't the Tamara she knew. Not this girl with bared teeth who was raising the oar again and letting out a low, threatening growl!

The dogs began to walk away. Soon, all three of them were loping up the slope to the trees.

"Now, where's that animal we saved?" Tamara asked, letting the oar fall to the ground.

Dodo struggled up and raced to the spot where she had last seen Darwin. Although the mud was etched with evidence of the battle, and the weeds on either side were dotted with feathers and fur, there was no sign of the bird.

"You told it to get in the water," Tamara reminded Dodo. "Can it swim?"

Shaking her head to indicate that she didn't know, Dodo started forward. The bottom of the bay sucked at her sneakers with every step. "Darwin!" she called, pushing at the grasses, rousing mosquitoes and gnats. "Darwin!"

When the water was lapping at her waist, Dodo saw a large gray shape floating just under the surface before her. Reaching down with both arms, she pulled.

"Uhhh . . ." breathed Darwin before he sank again.

"Quick," Dodo called. "Tamara! Over here! He's too heavy for me!"

Tamara splashed to Dodo's side. Together they groped under the water.

"We'll never lift him out," Tamara gasped. "He's too heavy. Just make sure his head surfaces."

Dodo nodded. "Right. I've got him."

The bird was dead weight in their arms. But he was breathing regularly, Dodo noted. He couldn't have swallowed much water. Reaching shore, they dropped him to the sand and then eased down next to him. For a full minute, the air was filled with their noisy panting. Gradually, another sound took over.

Ch-ch-ch-ch-ch-ch-ch-ch!

Listening to the clicking of cicadas, Tamara smiled. "I used to think they made the heat."

Dodo was confused. "What?"

"Those bugs. Do you hear them? I used to think they made the heat."

After the drama of the last ten minutes, the comment seemed ridiculous. "You thought that *bugs* made the heat?" Dodo faked a sneeze to cover up her laugh.

"I'd only hear them in the summer," Tamara explained. "When it was really hot. I guess they reminded me of our radiators."

"Why? Do yours clank?"

"Do they ever!"

"Ours do, too," Dodo said, forgetting that she was talking to a member of the Big Three, a person who presumably would not care about the Penny radiators. "Enough to wake you up at night."

"Look over there," another voice said, breaking into the conversation. "Don't you think that cloud looks like a package of Twinkle Pies?"

Spinning around, Tamara gasped. "This bird talks!"

Dodo clamped a hand across Tamara's mouth, as if putting a cork on the words would bottle up the discovery as well.

Think, she urged herself. What now?

CHAPTER 10

DARWIN DISCOVERED

"Doez it underztand what it'z zaying?"

Dodo released Tamara. In the matter of a split second, she decided to embark on a course of denial: she would act as if the bird had not spoken and Tamara had not heard it.

"I don't really like Twinkle Pies. Do you?" she asked. "They're awfully sweet."

"It talked," Tamara insisted, getting to her feet. "This bird talked, Dorothy Penny. And it didn't say, 'Polly want a cracker,' either."

"Would you *have* a cracker?" Darwin asked Tamara.

Dodo covered her face with her hands. So much for denial. She should have known that Darwin would not have enough sense to keep quiet.

Tamara moved to stand over the bird. "You'd better tell me what's going on, Dorothy. And don't say that you don't know anything. I heard you call it by name."

"That would be Darwin," Darwin offered helpfully.

Seeing no option other than the truth, Dodo lowered her hands to her lap and spoke weakly. "Can you keep a secret?"

"I'm the best at keeping secrets!" Tamara chortled. "Did you know that Gigi's mother's nails are all fake? I'm the only person Gigi told, and I've never told anyone."

"Except me."

"Except—? Whoops! You're right!"

Tamara seemed to think the slip was funny, but Dodo didn't share in the laughter. If Tamara were to tell about Darwin as easily as she'd told about Mrs. Bell's nails, Darwin's life could be in danger.

"You can't tell anyone," Dodo insisted. "Arley and I are the only ones who know about him. And you, now."

"I won't tell a soul," Tamara swore. "Not even Gigi's mother." She giggled again before asking, "What kind of animal is it, anyhow?"

"It's a dodo bird."

"Aren't they very rare?"

"They're sort of extinct. This one hatched in Aunt Hazel's bungalow, and Arley and I have been keeping him here."

"That's incredible!"

For so long, Dodo's main worry had been that Tamara would be horrified or disgusted by Darwin. But Tamara seemed to be interested. No. More than interested, Dodo decided. Excited. In fact, Tamara was wearing the same rapt expression she wore in Dodo's best daydreams!

"He's not too bright," Dodo went on, more eagerly, "but he does know what he's saying. Listen: who's helping you to change so that you can survive, Darwin?"

"You are," the bird responded promptly.

"Wow!"

Dodo grinned at Tamara's reaction.

"He doesn't seem to be changing enough, though, does he?" Tamara said. "Those dogs almost killed him. Old Darwin here didn't have a chance. Just what kind of bird is he supposed to change into?"

"Huh?"

"What is he supposed to imitate in order to survive?"

"I don't know," Dodo said as Tamara began walking around the bird. "I never thought about it that way."

"Some birds can fly. Some can swim, and some can run very fast. It's a cinch this one's not going to do all of that. You'd better concentrate on one area." Tamara stopped and looked at Dodo. "Why didn't you tell me about him before? Didn't you trust me?"

Dodo swallowed uneasily. "I—I didn't think you'd be interested."

"You've got to be kidding!" Tamara opened her eyes wide. "Who wouldn't be interested in a talking animal?"

"I don't know. Some people might think that it was . . . dumb or something. And if they didn't, they might want to put him in a zoo or a museum."

"If you knew me better, you'd know that you could trust me," Tamara said. "But I guess you don't. Know me, that is. Not yet, anyway. I don't know much about you, either. For instance, I never knew you had a nickname—"

Dodo was glad that Darwin chose that moment to speak.

"That cloud looks like a hot dog," he told Tamara, swiveling his head to see her. "With relish."

Taking advantage of the interruption to change the subject, Dodo retrieved her pad from her pocket. From the rescue, the pages were wet and stuck together. "I have a list of birds in the area. What you've got to do, Darwin, is decide which type appeals to you. Then study them as if your life depended on it."

"Because it might," Tamara added solemnly.

"So which will it be?" Dodo asked the bird. "The ducks? Or maybe the geese or the swans? How about the heron?"

Darwin gazed up raptly to where two gulls wheeled gracefully. "Them."

"Holy mackerel!" Tamara said. "He might as well try to be an elephant!"

The gulls were dropping what looked like stones onto the rocks below them. Swooping down, one bird began eating while another retrieved his object, flew up, and dropped it again. It took Dodo a minute to figure out that the gulls were cracking open their lunch: clams.

"Sea gulls don't sink," Tamara stated. "They can sit on the top of the water and paddle around. Also, they fly. They have these huge wings—"

Darwin interrupted her. "Do I still have to jog? I've never seen a gull jogging."

"Jog?" Tamara echoed.

Dodo tried to explain. "It's part of his survival lessons. Exercise and diet. I work with him every day. I don't suppose you'd want to help. . . ."

Tamara squealed. "Of course I would!"

"Really?"

Darwin was prodding Tamara with the tip of his wing. "Will you want me to teach you how to laugh, too?"

Hoping to cover the bird's words, Dodo spoke louder. "Arley and I meet Darwin here after breakfast. Then, after lunch—we bring our lunch did I tell you that? After lunch, we work on our projects a little bit—"

"What projects?" Tamara interrupted.

"Oh, something Aunt Hazel cooked up. And after one more jog on the beach, Arley and I head back to the lane and go swimming."

"It sounds terrific," Tamara said. "I'll just have to clear it with my parents." Saying that, she glanced around to the dinghy. "And we'd better get back to the boat or they'll think we were drowned. See you tomorrow, Darwin."

"See you!" Darwin sang out.

"Remember," Dodo told him as Tamara used an oar to push the dinghy back into the water. "Study the gulls. Do exactly what they do."

CHAPTER 11

FRIENDSHIP

Dodo waited until the next morning to tell Arley about Tamara. As she'd guessed, he wasn't happy.

"How do we know we can trust her?" he demanded as they sat down at the mouth of the lane to wait.

"Because she promised." And because Tamara is my friend, Dodo wanted to add. But was she? Did Tamara's interest in Darwin reflect an interest in Dodo as well?

"You'd better not do anything goofy," she warned her brother when she saw Tamara emerge from her bungalow and wave at them. "Not if Tamara can see."

"She'd better not do anything goofy, either," Arley retorted, "because I'll be watching her, too!"

Bag lunch in hand, Tamara hurried to where they were waiting, and then the three of them began the trek to the bay.

"Do you always come this route?" Tamara wanted to know as they entered the woods. "Wouldn't it be safer for Darwin if we varied it? You know, so that no one could follow us."

Arley's eyes lit up. "Hey, why didn't I think of that? Every day we can blaze a new trail. Let's try this way."

Although Dodo was relieved to see Arley put aside his distrust of Tamara, she was horrified when his new route involved a leap over a giant bush covered with burrs, as well as dead ends and backtracking. Third in line, she couldn't see Tamara's face. Was Tamara annoyed? Would she decide to go back home?

"Ta-da!" Arley trumpeted when he brought them finally to the edge of the woods. As he slipped down the incline to the bay beach, Tamara said, "Tomorrow *I* pick the trail."

Dodo wondered at the meaning of Tamara's words. Did she think being the leader would be fun, or did she want to choose a less demanding route?

On the beach, Arley was pointing. "Look at that!" he called. A bit of purple was gleaming up from the mud.

"What is it?" Tamara asked, rushing over to him.

By the time Dodo caught up, Arley had extracted a piece of purple glass and was holding it aloft.

"Isn't this a great color? What do you suppose it's from?"

"Perfume bottle?" Tamara guessed.

Dodo used her best older sister voice. "It's much too sharp to save, Arley. You'll cut yourself."

Ignoring her, Arley turned the purple glass over and over to examine all its facets. "You know, with a little eroding, this could be the prize of my whole collection. I'm gathering sea glass for my project," he explained to Tamara eagerly. "Sometime, I'll show it to you."

Dodo grimaced. Her warning had done no good at all! Here was Arley, acting as goofy as ever!

"If I could get this glass back into the bay," he said thoughtfully, "by the time it washed ashore again, it would be eroded."

"Oh, Arley!" Dodo said, rolling her eyes.

He was too busy examining the glass to notice. "You two go on ahead. I'm going to wade out to the edge of the reeds. I'll meet you in Crab City."

"What's Crab City?" Tamara asked.

Dodo took Tamara's arm and hurried her along. "It's just the spot in front of the drainage pipe where Darwin lives. Arley calls it that because you can see lots of fiddler crabs at low tide."

"Do they bite?"

"They don't want any part of you," Dodo assured her. "The worst part is trying not to step on them."

With the tide going out, Crab City was in what Arley called "rush hour." Tiny fiddler crabs, seemingly out for the sun, skittered for cover when Tamara positioned herself beside some tiger lilies and rotated in place. "I see the pipe, and I see the crabs. Where's Darwin?"

Remembering the dogs, Dodo was gripped by a horrible thought. Usually, the bird was waiting on the beach. Where could he be?

"Oh, there he is," Tamara announced.

Darwin was out amid the marsh grass, where the receding tide had uncovered a cluster of pewter gray rocks. Standing atop one of the larger ones with his tiny wings fluttering, he hadn't noticed the girls' arrival. As they approached, he stiffened his wings and let something fall from his mouth. Then, dipping down, he retrieved the object and stood up with wings flapping furiously.

"I think he's imitating the way the gulls drop clams onto rocks to open them," Dodo whispered. "He's doing it perfectly."

"Only he doesn't get off the ground," Tamara observed.

"*Ee-eu! Ee-eu!*" the bird cried, aping the call of the gulls. "Drat," he mumbled as the thing he had been dropping rolled off the rock and into the mud.

"What do you have there?" Dodo asked.

Startled, Darwin slid off the rock sidewards. "Oh, hi!" he said, sounding a bit strained. "I thought it was earlier. I was just getting my breakfast."

"Breakfast?"

In the mud before Dodo lay a can of MacaroniOs.

Darwin puffed out his feathers. "I was trying to do what the gulls do. I'm following your instructions, aren't I?"

"Where did you get that can?" Dodo demanded. "You know you aren't supposed to eat people food. You have to survive on whatever you can find."

With his feathers still sticking out, Darwin waddled protectively around the can. "What are you going to do with my MacaroniOs? Will you eat them?"

"Of course not. I guess I'll throw them out."

"Throw them out?" Darwin gasped, and his feathers dropped down flat. "Oh. I feel weak!"

Tamara waved her hands rapidly in front of the bird's face. "Maybe he'd better eat the stuff, Dorothy. We wouldn't want him to faint or anything. And besides, he did find the can by himself. It must have washed ashore from a boat. It seems like fair game."

Looking at the bird's glistening eyes, Dodo relented. "All right. I guess you can eat the MacaroniOs, Darwin. They're not going to help you lose weight, though."

Darwin didn't seem to care. He punctured the lid of the can with his sharp beak and set about eating.

"It's going to be hot today," Dodo forecast, lifting her hair off her neck and scanning the cloudless sky. "Nineties. We'd better jog first thing, before the sun gets too strong."

"You said you'd let me help," Tamara reminded Dodo. "What can I do?"

"You can be in charge of the warm-up."

Setting her lunch on one of the rocks, Tamara positioned herself in front of the bird and waited until he had cleaned the last of the pasta Os from the can. "Watch me," she instructed. "First, lift your toes like this. That will keep you from getting shin splints."

Even though Dodo wasn't sure whether or not Darwin had shins, she encouraged him to do as Tamara suggested. Knowing that the bird could only balance with both feet planted firmly on the ground, she moved to his rear, and prepared to right him if he began to topple.

"Now stretch your leg to the back, like this," Tamara said, demonstrating. "Don't bounce. Just stretch."

Darwin lifted his leg as told, thrusting all his weight forward. Dodo just managed to rush around in time to catch him.

"That's enough for today," she decided. "Darwin's not too good on the exercises. He's better at running. I'll lead the way."

Tamara jumped up in readiness. "Race you to that big bush up ahead!"

Torn between her desire to please Tamara and her plans for Darwin, Dodo hesitated.

"Come on," Tamara taunted. "I'll take a five second handicap, if you're afraid of losing."

"I'm not afraid of losing. On your mark, get set, go!"

Being in a better starting position, Tamara had the initial advantage. With Dodo on her heels, she tacked back and forth, trying to avoid the crabs. But when Tamara reached the straight strip of beach, Dodo, with her longer legs, quickly caught up and flew on past to reach the bush with a good two-stride lead.

"I'll . . . beat you . . . next time," Tamara panted.

"No . . . you won't!" Dodo panted back.

Leaning on each other for support, the two girls staggered to Hamburger Rock, where Arley sat talking about television with Darwin.

"Did you watch 'Hospital Zone' for me?" Darwin asked.

"How can I? It's on at lunchtime, when I'm with you."

"What do you want to know?" Tamara said. "Sometimes I watch that soap opera."

Darwin wriggled his tail with pleasure. "What's been happening to Hortense? It's been weeks since I tuned in."

"She's getting married."

"To Doctor Walden?"

"No, to a nurse."

Something in Darwin's throat moved up and down, ruffling the feathers on his neck. "Not the one that mixed up the medicines and put Hortense's brother into a coma!"

Laughing, Arley patted Darwin on the back. "Hey, it's only make-believe."

"And anyway, Darwin," Tamara went on, "I don't think the wedding's going to come off. Hortense's brother opened his eyes in the last episode I saw."

"But what if Hortense's brother doesn't recover until *after* the wedding?" Dodo asked. "Then Hortense will find out that she's married to a murderer!"

"But Hortense's brother didn't die," Arley said. "So the nurse isn't a murderer. He's a . . . a . . . what do you call someone who puts somebody into a coma?"

"A comedian?" Darwin tried.

All three children burst into laughter.

"No," Tamara sputtered. "You're the comedian, Darwin!"

"So what are we going to do?" Arley asked. "Want to play something?"

Dodo shook her head frantically. Tamara wouldn't want to *play!* She had come along expecting to help train Darwin. Why didn't Arley ever think before he spoke?

"How about Twenty Questions?" Arley suggested.

"May I be the game show host?" Darwin asked. "Pretty please? Hamburger Rock can be my desk."

"I'll go first," Tamara said, taking a place beside the bird. "I've got a person in mind."

Arley settled down on one side of the rock. Reluctantly, Dodo sat down opposite him.

"You won the toss backstage, Arley," Darwin intoned. "We'll start the questioning with you."

"Are you thinking of a man?"

"Nope," Tamara answered.

"One down," Darwin said, "and we go to Dodo. Remember, you're playing for the washer-dryer combination!"

Dodo sent Tamara a sidelong glance.

"Hurry up," Darwin urged. "Time is running out Soon we'll have to break for a message from our sponsor."

"Are you thinking of a woman?" Dodo asked.

"Yes," Tamara replied. "A female, anyway."

"Are you thinking of somebody who's dead?"

"No."

Darwin tapped the rock with his bill. "Three down, and control of the game moves to Arley."

"Are you thinking of somebody we know?" Arley demanded.

"Yes."

"Are you thinking of one of your friends?"

"Yes."

"I don't know any of your friends!" Arley complained.

"You know this one," Tamara said mysteriously.

Arley sighed. "Are you thinking of that girl—what's her name—Barbie?"

"Barbie Fishbein," Dodo interjected.

"Nope."

Darwin nodded at Dodo. "Six down."

"Are you thinking of Gigi Bell?"

Again, Tamara shook her head negatively.

"I've got it!" Arley exclaimed. "You're thinking of Dodo!"

"Ding ding ding ding!" Tamara chanted. "You win!"

"And Dodo loses!" Arley teased.

A smile spread slowly across Dodo's face. She was Tamara's friend! Tamara had said so.

"Don't feel too bad."

Dodo looked up to see Darwin holding one wing out in an awkward handshake gesture. "I'm sure we have a nice consolation prize for you," the bird said.

"Like what?" Arley wanted to know. "What does Dodo get?"

"What do you want?" Tamara asked her.

Dodo thought for a moment. "Nothing, really. Except . . . Darwin knows what I want."

The bird fluffed his feathers, then smoothed them again. "I do? Is it something to eat?"

"Are we playing the game again?" Arley demanded. "Because if we are, it's supposed to be my turn to think of something. I did win, you know."

Dodo shook her head. "We're not playing. What I want from Darwin is for him to work hard at his lessons and imitate the other birds."

"I will," Darwin vowed. "I'll work so hard you won't know me!"

CHAPTER 12

≻═══≺

THE RETURN
OF
THE BIG THREE

"Guess what?" Tamara asked Dodo and Arley one morning as they started for the bay.

Glancing at the shopping bag Tamara was carrying, Dodo said, "You brought lemonade for us."

"Nope."

"You didn't bring lemonade," Arley said.

"I didn't, but that's not it. It's something really good."

"What? What?" Dodo asked impatiently.

Tamara jumped up and down as they crossed the street. "My father went home this morning!"

Arley was studying the bag. "You really didn't bring lemonade?"

"My father went home," Tamara repeated, "and when he comes back on Friday, he's bringing Barbie and Gigi with him!"

It seemed to Dodo that the macadam beneath her feet gave way suddenly, plunging her into a dark pit. She had just stopped worrying about whether Tamara liked her or not. What would happen when

Tamara's old friends arrived? Would Tamara forget about her?

"I wish you'd brought lemonade," Arley said. "I'm tired of apple juice."

"It's going to be great, Dorothy," Tamara predicted. "We'll have so much fun. But of course, we won't be able to visit with Darwin while they're here. Darwin is our secret."

Our secret. The words gave Dodo a thrill. Tamara liked her. There was no reason the other members of the Big Three wouldn't like her, too. Was there?

"My mother is planning a barbecue," Tamara went on. "You're both invited. Your Aunt Hazel, too."

"May I plan something special?" For the first time in a long while, the Big Three had returned to Dodo's imagination.

"You're a wonderful hostess, Dorothy," Barbie said.

"I've never had a better time in my life," Gigi purred. *"Don't you think we should make Dorothy the Big Fourth?"*

"Sure," the real Tamara answered. "Plan anything you like."

All week Dodo thought about what she could do to win over Barbie and Gigi. In the end, she convinced Aunt Hazel to give her enough money to take the Big Three to Davy Jones's Locker for lunch.

Friday morning seemed interminable to Dodo. After Arley set off for the preserve, she stationed herself at one of the bungalow windows to wait. She waited. And she waited, all the while growing more and more nervous. Why hadn't Tamara accepted her invitation for them to wait together? Did Tamara really have to clean, as she had said? Or had she wanted to be rid of Dodo before her "real" friends arrived?

When Dodo finally saw a flash of color at the top of the lane, she flew out of the bungalow, calling ahead, "Hi! Hi! I'm taking you to lunch!"

"Dorothy Penny," Barbie said. "What are you doing here?"

A familiar sick feeling passed through Dodo. "Uh, I'm staying with my aunt . . . in that bungalow . . . over there."

Above their bright red and yellow sun dresses, Gigi's and Barbie's faces blossomed into smiles. For a moment, Dodo was relieved. She grinned back, only realizing then that neither girl was looking at her. They had seen Tamara.

"Come down to the beach," Tamara called, taking them all in with a wave of her arm. "Daddy, please take their bags."

Within moments, Gigi, Barbie, and Tamara were running for the seawall and stairs.

"Aren't you going, too?" Mr. Hughes asked Dodo, shifting his briefcase to the arm that carried a bag of groceries so that he could pick up the two overnight cases.

Dodo felt as though she'd eaten something heavy for breakfast. Cannonballs with syrup. "Oh," she said. "Sure."

It just wasn't enough to be Dorothy Penny, she told herself, starting for the beach. She should have had her hair styled. She should have asked for a new outfit. And while she was at it, she thought, she should have developed a whole new personality.

At the top of the staircase, Dodo paused: if someone were drowning, she could perform a daring rescue! Her spirits rising, she searched the Sound for swimmers in trouble. There! Someone flailing her arms! It was . . . it was Miss Milton. Dodo's scheme came crashing down. Miss Milton was an able swimmer, if awkward. And it was probably fortunate, Dodo decided, since she wasn't at all sure she could save anyone so big.

"What are you waiting for, Dorothy?" Tamara called. "Come on!"

Tamara's radio was playing loudly. As Dodo went down the steps, she watched all three girls swaying to the music, their movements synchronous.

"Ah-hem," she coughed at the bottom, wanting to make her presence known.

Gigi giggled. "Bless you."

Tamara began moving her arms from side to side.

The other girls followed suit. "Are you getting a cold?" she asked Dodo.

"Back and forth," Barbie instructed. Tamara and Gigi changed their steps to match hers.

Trying to fit in, Dodo snapped her fingers and moved her feet. The constant shift of movements was a routine that the other girls were obviously familiar with, but Dodo found it impossible to keep up. After a minute, she coughed again.

"I don't know about anybody else, but I'm starved. Let's go back to the bungalows and get ready for lunch. We're all going to a restaurant called Davy Jones's Locker, my treat."

Tamara reached down to shut off the radio.

"Isn't Davy Jones's locker at the bottom of the ocean?" Gigi asked.

"To go there, don't you have to be"—Barbie drew a finger across her neck—"dead?"

"No," Tamara laughed. "You eat the food and *then* you meet Davy Jones." Sticking her tongue out of the side of her mouth, she finished, "Food poisoning!"

Dodo smiled uncertainly, watching Barbie and Gigi run back up the wooden staircase, whispering in each other's ears. They didn't seem nearly as excited as she had hoped they would be at the prospect of an outing.

"I have to do something," she told herself, standing before the mirror in Aunt Hazel's bathroom, staring at her face, with its freckles and fringe of wild hair.

But what? Did she dare laugh for Barbie with Barbie's laugh? Could she turn Gigi's smile on Gigi? Gigi's teeth were like pearls on a string, even and all in line, Dodo thought, grinning at her reflection to study the effect. Her own were more like the shingles on the bungalow. Jagged and uneven.

Lowering her top lip, Dodo patted her face into place and went out to meet the girls in the lane. Tamara had put a dress on, too. Dodo felt conspicuous in her faded shorts.

"Well," she said, trying to talk like a ventriloquist in order to keep her lips from exposing her teeth.

"Well," echoed Gigi. She looked at Barbie and tittered.

Tamara started the group walking up the lane. "The place Dorothy's taking us to is a really great restaurant. You can get burgers or franks. And they have super fried clams. I'm going to have a vanilla shake and a hamburger. What about you, Dorothy?"

"Uh, the same," Dodo said, still stiff lipped.

Gigi stuck her elbow into Barbie's side.

"I thought you liked chocolate shakes better," Tamara said.

Everything had a dreamy quality to Dodo. She shook her head, trying to wake up. "Oh. I do, don't I?"

"Then why would you get vanilla?" Barbie asked.

"Did I say vanilla?" Dodo smacked her head. "Chocolate, chocolate! I'm having chocolate!"

This time, all three of the other girls laughed. A single, high-pitched note was sounding in Dodo's ears, an alarm that she didn't know how to turn off.

"I went to see the best movie," Barbie started.

Dodo couldn't keep her mind on the words. She kept watching the shift of eyes: Barbie to Tamara; Tamara to Barbie, then Gigi; Gigi to Barbie. Had they forgotten she was there? Why didn't anyone look at her? When Barbie finished talking, Dodo tossed her head back and laughed. "Ha-ha-ha-*hee*-ha."

At last, Dodo had captured their gazes. She swallowed uneasily. It wasn't at all as she had imagined.

"That's the boardwalk just up ahead," Tamara told Barbie and Gigi. "Maybe, after we're done eating, we can play some video games or get ice cream cones."

Dodo felt for the money in her pocket. Would she have enough to buy lunch *and* ice cream? How much did each game cost?

"Is this the place we're going to?" Gigi reached out to touch a sign that hung at the beginning of the boardwalk:

DAVY JONES'S LOCKER
Now Open 7 Days a Week, Year-Round
Come in and Cool off in Our
New, Centrally Air-Conditioned Rooms!

"This is it!" Dodo confirmed. "Want to sit inside or out here?"

The front of the building was mostly glass, revealing a large, dim room that looked both cool and crowded. A television was playing above the beverage counter. Dodo recognized the face of Hortense from "Hospital Zone." Hortense was wearing a wedding dress.

Tamara nodded at the cluster of tables on the boardwalk. "We'd probably get served quicker out here. And we could watch the people on the beach. How about that table, with the yellow umbrella?"

Anxious to get the seat next to Tamara, Dodo rushed over, accidentally knocking heads with Gigi. "Oops," she said, stepping back onto Barbie's foot.

"I know," Gigi said. "Dorothy can sit out here, and we'll go inside."

"Ha-*hee*-ha-ha-ha," Barbie laughed.

She'd had the laugh all wrong, Dodo realized. "Ha-HEE-ha-ha-ha," she joined in. In the wake of the laugh came absolute silence. Embarrassed, Dodo looked down at the table top.

"Do you need menus?" The waiter who appeared was wearing an apron over shorts. He held out four miniature oars that were covered with writing. "Today's soup is clam chowder, and the special is Locker Shrimp. That's shrimp, breaded and deep fried, in a basket."

Gigi smiled, showing off her pretty teeth. "I think we know what we want. I'll have a burger, fries, and a root beer."

"A burger and a vanilla shake," Tamara said.

Barbie nodded. "Same for me."

"Me too," Dodo added, concentrating so that her teeth remained hidden. She didn't understand why the other girls stared at her until the waiter was on his way back into the building.

"Make that chocolate," she shouted. "Waiter! Make that last shake chocolate."

"You'd better go inside to make sure he heard you," Barbie suggested.

Dodo felt foolish. "It's all right. I'll drink whatever he brings me."

"That's dumb," Gigi said. "If you want chocolate, get chocolate."

It was turning out all wrong, Dodo thought. Whatever was the matter? Why couldn't she turn herself into a girl the Big Three would like?

"Maybe Dorothy really doesn't care," Tamara said.

Dodo sent Tamara a grateful smile, which quickly wilted when Tamara turned back to the other girls.

"So when do we get to see this yacht of yours?" Barbie asked.

"Is it really a yacht?" Dodo said, speaking louder than she needed to. "I mean, how big does a boat have to be before it's a yacht?"

"Tomorrow," Tamara said. "First thing in the morning, we'll go out on the boat."

"Does it have a—a what-do-you-call-it, a head?" Gigi asked.

"Isn't that what you call the bathroom?" Dodo interjected.

Tamara was answering Gigi. "Yes, and there's a table with benches."

Feeling as if she would evaporate into the summer sky if Tamara didn't remember her soon, Dodo sought something to attract Tamara's attention. Hardly knowing what she was saying, she blurted, "Do you like birds, Barbie?"

"For what?" Barbie asked. "To, like, eat?"

"No, as pets."

Dodo felt someone's foot kick her under the table.

"Barbie's father *raises* birds," Tamara said, applying another kick to Dodo's shin. "He breeds them. In cages. For money."

"Actually, I think birds are pretty dumb," Barbie announced. "I mean, they look okay when they're free and flying, but when they're in cages, they can't fly, and all they do is mess up the papers. The ones on the bottom of the cage. You know?"

Gigi made a face. "We know. Icky."

"Listen, you guys," Tamara said in a rush of words. "Dorothy's got a nickname."

Dodo couldn't believe her ears!

"Tell them," Tamara prodded Dodo. "Tell them what your brother calls you."

Dodo pushed her chair back. She shook her head.

"He calls her Dodo," Tamara said. "Isn't that—Hey! Where are you going?"

Dodo had gotten up from her seat so fast that the chair had tipped over backwards. As she spun around to get away, she ran headfirst into the waiter, who was bringing their drinks.

"Watch it!" he shouted, too late.

The root beer and the three vanilla shakes bounced up into the air and came crashing down on both the waiter and Dodo.

CHAPTER 13

⊶

EXTINCTION

Dodo hugged her legs and pressed her back against the cold, damp wall of the drainage pipe. She felt safe with nothing to see but a circle of reeds and sand and sky, with nothing to hear but a faraway trickling of water draining from somewhere unseen.

Her life was over, she thought, feeling tears mix with the root beer on her cheeks. She could never face the Big Three again. She would have to move, have to start a new life.

The air around the pipe was sweet. Taking in a breath in a series of little, spasmodic gulps, Dodo reached out to pluck a pink flower that was growing at the edge of the cement pipe. In surprise, she drew her hand back and sucked at the hole a thorn had made. The simple, four-petaled roses that grew on the beach were pretty and fragrant, but their bushes were studded with spikes.

Just like life, Dodo thought miserably. She pressed on the cut until it stopped bleeding and then exhaled in one long sigh.

The Big Three didn't want her, she told herself. They didn't want her any more than a tricycle wanted a fourth wheel. They didn't want her any more than . . . than Darwin wanted his diet of berries and fish. What use was she, anyhow?

That thought made Dodo break down. For a while, she sobbed without control, appreciating the way the sorrowful sound echoed through the yards of pipe. Then, her tears spent, she stared into the darkness behind her. Sniffing, she wiped her eyes dry with the sides of her hands. What was piled up there, along the curved wall? No. Not piled. Neatly stacked. Arranged like a display in a supermarket.

"*Cans!*" Dodo said aloud.

Cans were stockpiled in the drainage pipe! MacaroniOs. Tomato soup. Peaches. Fruity-ade.

"This stuff didn't wash ashore from any boat," Dodo said, knocking cans to the left and right as she sprang from the pipe to stomp across the strip of beach. "No wonder Darwin isn't losing weight.

"Darwin!" she shouted to the bay. "Where are you?"

The tide was rising. Dodo saw it sweep forward and spiral down into the homes of Crab City. As each hole filled, a circle of foam floated up, and when the caves were covered, they became invisible beneath the water of the bay.

"I know you're around here somewhere," Dodo shouted, squinting her eyes to protect them from the glare coming off the water. "You can't hide from me, Darwin!"

Where was that dumb dodo?

"*Ee-eu!*"

There he was. The bird was sitting on one of the taller rocks out in the marsh grass. Dodo could just see the top of his gray head. He was facing away from her, hoping, she figured, to remain unseen.

"You promised that you would imitate the gulls," she said, feeling fury rise in her. "How do you expect to survive? You cheater!"

The bird blinked and ruffled his feathers.

"Did you hear me, Darwin?"

At the edge of the water, Dodo hesitated, wondering whether or not to get her sneakers wet.

"You're going to wind up like all the other dodos!" she cried. "Extinct! *Extinct!*"

The bird turned then, as if to see what the fuss was about. When he saw Dodo, he jumped down from the rock and pressed into the reeds.

Despite the summer heat, Dodo shivered. She'd noticed something when her eyes had met with the bird's. There had been no sign of understanding there. No hungry dodo, no silly Darwin. *Nothing.*

"Wait," she called out. "Come back! I'm not mad anymore. I don't want you to be like a gull. I don't want you to be like a duck or a heron, either. I only want you to be you! Darwin, come back!"

The bird was gone. With the instincts of a wild

creature, he had put distance between himself and one of his predators.

The lessons had not been in vain, Dodo realized. Darwin was going to survive. But the bird she had known and loved was extinct, just the same.

CHAPTER 14

EVOLUTION

"Thanks a lot!"

At the voice, Dodo looked up from the dust her sneakers had been making as she'd scraped her feet through the dried dirt of the lane. She wasn't sure just how long she'd sat on the bay beach, hoping to get another glimpse of the bird Darwin had become, but it had been long enough for all thoughts of the Big Three to have left her mind.

"I love being invited out to eat and then left with the bill," Tamara added sarcastically. "Especially when I don't bring money with me."

Dodo closed her eyes, warding off tears.

"I had to call my father to bail us out," Tamara went on. "Some friend you are, Dorothy Penny."

It was only after Tamara had spun around and was striding toward the seawall that Dodo found words. "I'll pay your father back," she offered. "I'll apologize to Barbie and Gigi! I'll . . . I'll . . ."

Finding herself alone again, Dodo kicked at the ground, sending up a small brown cloud. Could anyone have made a bigger mess of things than she had? Dragging the toes of her shoes, she scuffed toward the bungalow.

"There you are, Dodo," Aunt Hazel said, appearing in the doorway with her straw hat on her head and a wraparound skirt over her bathing suit. "What have you got all over you?"

Dodo rubbed halfheartedly at the sticky drink on her face. "Dirt."

"It's time we were going to the Hugheses' party. I already sent Arley on down."

Dodo had forgotten about the barbecue. "I don't want to go," she said. As she moved to cross the threshold, Aunt Hazel laid a hand on her forehead.

"You feeling okay?"

For the first time that summer, Dodo felt homesick. She longed for the comforting presence of her mother. "I tried to impress some girls and wound up looking like a fool," she wanted to say. "I tried to buy two friends and wound up losing the one I had. I told a very special bird how he ought to act and turned him into something boringly ordinary. I don't feel okay, I feel wretched!"

But Mrs. Penny was miles away.

"I'm fine," Dodo told Aunt Hazel. "I just don't feel like going."

Aunt Hazel would hear none of it. "I don't know what went on at that restaurant, but I do know that, whatever it was, you can't run away from it. Get yourself cleaned up. Ten minutes!"

Knowing that her aunt was not one to be trifled with, Dodo went on into the bungalow, timing herself carefully so as not to appear either late or a minute sooner than she needed to. When she arrived on the beach, she was freshly showered and in her best bathing suit.

"Dodo plays with us," Arley said when he saw her.

Some distance from where the grown-ups hovered over Aunt Hazel's three-legged barbecue, a volleyball net had been strung up. On one side stood Barbie and Gigi, and on the other Arley and Tamara. From the downcast expression on Arley's face, Dodo had no trouble knowing which team was winning.

"No fair, Arley," Gigi argued. "That'll give you three people to our two."

"Dodo plays with us," Tamara echoed. "Barbie is twice as good as anybody else. Dodo will even things up."

Wincing at Tamara's use of her nickname, Dodo moved into place beside her brother, up close to the net, facing Barbie.

"Let's play," she said.

Back at the makeshift serving line, Gigi swung her arm back and knuckled the ball into the air. Dodo watched it go high, so high that it seemed to scrape against the deep blue of the sky.

"Get it, get it!" Arley screamed as the ball arced back to earth. Dodo was mesmerized by its approach. "Play, you dummy," Arley shouted. Then, shoving Dodo roughly aside, he popped the ball back to Barbie, who easily spiked it to the pebbles at Dodo's feet.

"Point!" Gigi called.

"Seven-nothing," Arley told Dodo through gritted teeth.

Volleyball was something Dodo understood. Awakening to the challenge, she ran and stretched and stooped to return the ball. Back and forth over the net it sailed, and for a wonderful time, the ball was the only thing that existed for Dodo. Almost single-handedly, she began to even the score.

"Dodo Dodo Dodo," Arley chanted.

"Dodo Dodo," Tamara joined in.

The score was ten-eight when Mr. Hughes interrupted the game. "Tamara! Run up to the bungalow!" he called. "Get more ice, please. We're almost ready to eat."

"Ketchup and napkins, too," Mrs. Hughes ordered, pushing at the thick gray smoke rising from the barbecue. "Better take somebody with you."

Groaning with disappointment, Arley dropped to the ground.

"You were saved by the bell," Barbie told him.

Gigi added, "From a humiliating defeat."

"We were going to win!"

"But you didn't," Barbie retorted. "And since we

were ahead—throughout the entire game, I might add—we win."

"We don't concede," Arley shouted. "We challenge you to a . . . a . . . what do you call it? A tiebreaker!"

"But it wasn't a tie!"

Tamara spoke quickly. "Maybe we can finish the game later. Pick up where we left off. Is that all right with everyone?"

"Aww," Barbie cooed. "Little Miss Peacemaker to the rescue."

Tamara pasted on a sweet smile. "It's a dirty job, but somebody has to do it. Especially around you two!" As she rushed to the steps, she nodded at Dodo. "Come help."

Surprised, Dodo trotted after her. Up the staircase. Past the oak tree. Onto the Hugheses' porch. Finally Dodo found the courage to speak.

"How come you wanted me? Aren't you mad?"

Tamara was leading the way through the living room. "I was. Anybody would be. And if you put Darwin in danger again, I'll stay mad."

For a moment, Dodo recalled the bird's blank eyes. Pushing that thought away, she followed Tamara through the dining room and into the kitchen. "Well, you know, I should be mad, too. You were ready to spend my money on ice cream and video games."

"If you didn't have enough, you should have said something."

"And look like a jerk in front of Barbie and Gigi?"

"You were doing that already."

"Well, you didn't have to go and make fun of me!"

Tamara's face softened. "I never made fun of you."

"Yes, you did. You told Barbie and Gigi my nickname."

"I had to do something to change the subject. You were going to tell about Darwin. Remember? And what's wrong with your nickname, anyhow?"

"It's . . . it's . . ."

"It's cute," Tamara finished. "I only told them because I thought they'd like it. I mean, your aunt calls you Dodo, and your brother calls you Dodo. I figured if I was really your friend, you'd want me to call you Dodo, too." She opened the freezer and pulled out an ice tray. "But maybe you don't consider me your friend."

With a loud *ca-runch*, she emptied the tray into a bucket.

"Do you mean we can be friends again?" Dodo asked.

Tamara slammed the freezer door shut with her elbow. "We never stopped being friends, did we? Is there some kind of rule that we can't ever be mad at each other? Don't you get angry with Arley?"

"Sure."

"And then don't you forgive him and play with him again?"

"Yeah."

Having made her point, Tamara smiled. "So there."

"Is it because I played volleyball—"

Picking up an ice cube, Tamara tossed it to Dodo. The cube bounced out of Dodo's hands and slid under the stove. "I don't care how you play volleyball. I only care about how fast you can run. Beat you back to the beach."

All of a sudden, Dodo felt absurdly happy. "I have to get the ketchup and stuff."

"No excuses. On your mark, get set, go!"

Grabbing the napkins from the counter, Dodo whipped the refrigerator door open to search for the ketchup. With the large plastic bottle clutched in one hand, she started after Tamara.

"You lose, you lose!" Tamara was hollering as she took the steps two at a time.

On the beach, they ran, neck and neck, toward the barbecue, where Mr. Hughes put out his arms to stop them.

"Watch the fire!" he cautioned.

"I beat you," Tamara claimed, laughing.

"No, you didn't," Dodo insisted. "It was a tie. Wasn't it, Mr. Hughes?"

Tamara's father shook his head, refusing to get involved. "Better eat the food while it's hot. Your friends over there have already been served."

Barbie and Gigi were seated near the water. Taking paper plates and piling them with food, Tamara and Dodo joined them.

"So why aren't you on the school volleyball team?" Tamara asked Dodo as they settled down.

"I don't know. Nobody ever asked me."

"Nobody ever asked me, either," Barbie said. "And you're a better player than I am. Do you always wait for formal invitations?"

Gigi laughed, then said, "*I* wait for formal invitations, Dorothy. And I only respond to engraved ones. Why does your brother call you Dodo? Does it have anything to do with leaving restaurants before your food arrives?"

"What do they say?" Barbie asked. " 'Dumb as a dodo'?"

Dodo wiped her mouth and mumbled into a paper napkin. " 'Dead as a dodo.' "

"I wish I had a nickname," Tamara mused.

Barbie waved her fork in the air. "We'll give you one! Come on, Gigi, think!"

"Tammy."

"Oh, that's boring," Barbie complained.

Tamara grabbed her napkin as it was lifted by a breeze. "I have an idea. Let's give ourselves nicknames. Secret nicknames, that are just for us to use."

Barbie spoke in an exaggerated fashion, leaving Dodo to wonder whether or not she was serious.

"What a *good* idea. Why don't we make them *animal* names, to go along with Dorothy's—I mean, *Dodo*'s. What could Gigi's be?"

"Kitty?" Tamara suggested.

Gigi leaned over to Tamara and spoke in a loud whisper. "Barbie can be Hyena!"

"What did you say?" Barbie asked, narrowing her eyes. "I heard that, Gigi."

"I think Tamara should be Birdie. Or Turtle."

"If you said what I think you said, Gigi Bell, you're in trouble!" Barbie threatened.

"Mouse," Gigi proposed. "Tamara can be Mouse!"

"Ha-*hee*-ha-ha-ha!" Barbie laughed. "Oh, definitely. Mouse is perfect for Tamara."

"I guess I am kind of small," Tamara admitted, folding her used plate. "And my hair is brown, and I am quiet— Well, I am, aren't I? Sometimes?"

"Ha-*hee*-ha-ha-ha!"

Tamara slapped Barbie's arm playfully with her compacted garbage. "Finish eating, Hyena. I want to go swimming."

It was too confusing for Dodo. Listening to the Big Three was like getting on a merry go round and being swung until you were so dizzy you couldn't see straight, she thought. Did Barbie and Gigi like her? Did they even like each other?

At Aunt Hazel's insistence, no one entered the water for thirty minutes, to allow time for food to digest. By then, the sun was nudging the horizon.

Dodo felt there was something special about swimming so late in the day. As the sun dipped down, the air cooled, and the water was as warm and soothing as a bath. The atmosphere, however, was anything but relaxed.

"Barbie swims like a giraffe," Gigi shouted to Tamara. "Hey, Barbie! Are you afraid to get your hair wet?"

"Stop it!" Barbie complained as Arley began decorating her with seaweed. "And don't splash, Tamara!"

As the Big Three dissolved into screams, Dodo dove down to enter a murky world where sound was muffled and light was muted. Opening her eyes, she strained to see around her. On one side, eight skinny legs of varying lengths hopped about. On the other, three sets of thicker, adult legs plowed the water.

Turning away from them all, Dodo exhaled and forced herself down toward the bottom. There were legs there, too. Black ones, splayed from a round body. In its crude simplicity, the creature looked prehistoric.

A spider crab, Dodo decided, watching it creep along the sand. If it noticed the girl suspended above it, it didn't care, she thought. It was content in its ignorance of her, and of life above the waves, the Big Three included.

Bursting up into the world of air and noise, Dodo was just in time to hear Mr. Hughes announce, "Marshmallow time! Scout around for sticks!"

In the evening air, Dodo felt chilled. She wrapped herself in a dry, scratchy towel, then went after Arley. "I have to talk to you," she called.

Arley was heading for some scrubby-looking bushes. He waited for her to catch up.

"It's about Darwin," she said.

"What about him?"

"He's—he's changing, Arley." She had decided to break the news slowly.

Arley stopped to pick up a branch that had washed ashore. "Isn't that what you wanted?"

"If Darwin changes," Dodo said carefully, "he won't be Darwin anymore."

Arley didn't react. He stripped the twigs and bark from the stick, then cracked it in two over his knee and handed one half to Dodo.

"No matter what I thought ought to happen," Dodo went on, "I realized today that I don't want Darwin to stop being Darwin. I only want him to survive."

The light was nearly drained from the sky. In the east, stars were twinkling. Arley moved closer to peer hard into his sister's eyes. "Let me get this straight. You don't care anymore if he doesn't change?"

"I don't want him to change," she answered. As Arley let out a whoop, Dodo pressed on his arm to calm him. "It's too late. He did change!"

"I don't see why he would have," Arley said, shaking himself loose. "I've been giving him food—people food, that is—and he never really exercised the way you wanted him to—"

Remembering the stash of cans in the drainage pipe, Dodo frowned. "That was underhanded, Arley."

Arley shrugged. "I only wanted Darwin to survive."

"Do you suppose it isn't too late? Do you think that maybe we can find him tomorrow and turn him back into the silly bird he was when we met him?"

Arley started walking toward the barbecue. Tamara, Gigi, and Barbie were gathered around the charcoal embers, already loading sticks with marshmallows. "We don't have to find him, Dodo. I know where he is."

"You do?"

Arley swung his stick through the air, fighting invisible enemies. "Darwin and I walked down the bay beach toward the restaurants and arcades this afternoon. We had ice cream. I left him behind Davy Jones's Locker."

Dodo grabbed Arley's stick as it whooshed past her head. "You mean he wasn't by the drainage pipe? It wasn't Darwin that I saw disappear into the reeds?"

"You must have been looking at that coot," Arley said, grinning hugely. "I guess you're not as observant as you thought!"

Impulsively, Dodo threw her arms around her brother, hugging him as she hadn't done since he was a baby.

"Cut it out!" he cried.

"Oh, Arley," she said. "You were such a creep to undermine my plans for Darwin. I love you!"

CHAPTER 15

THE BEGINNING OF AN IDEA

The next morning, after seven games of checkers, three of war, and forty-six of tic-tac-toe, Dodo and Arley went out on the porch to search for blue patches in the sky. Thunder had been rumbling all morning, keeping them inside.

"Darwin really is all right," Dodo said, making the words sound more like a question than a statement. "You're sure he was down by the restaurant yesterday and not by the drainage pipe."

"I'm sure."

"And you think he'll have found food and a place to sleep."

When a flash of white zigzagged across the sky, Dodo counted. One, two . . . The thunder cracked sharply. Why didn't the storm move on?

Backing up from the screen, Arley began poking around in the clutter. "Stop worrying. Darwin probably walked back to the pipe the minute the rain started."

Dodo settled herself atop the pile of life jackets

and propped her chin in her hands. It was one thing to decide that Darwin shouldn't change. It was something else to figure out how he would survive without changing.

"*Cheep, cheep. Cheep cheep!*"

Dodo squinted through the screen as Barbie's voice whispered, "That's not a mouse sound, dopey. That's a bird!"

Amid giggles, something bounced off the step in front of the bungalow.

"Did you see that?" Arley asked.

Dodo opened the door to look about. She was just in time to see an umbrella disappear into the Hughes bungalow. The lane itself was empty, except for a small white box just beyond the base of the porch stoop. Using an oar that had been propped in a corner of the porch, Dodo dragged the box close enough to grab, getting drenched in the process.

"It's private," she announced, reading what was written on the muddied lid: *For Dodo's Eyes Only.* Inside was a folded piece of paper.

Dear Dodo,
I can't believe it's raining! Gigi and Barbie
are leaving tomorrow, and it's raining!
We're going absolutely crazy (and so is my
mother) and have decided to go to a mall.
Would you like to come? While you're
asking your aunt, you might ask about

*tonight as well. Do you think you could
come for dinner and sleep over? We don't
have a bed for you, but you can bring a
pillow and blanket. And anyway we don't
sleep! We're nocturnal animals. (Remember
Mouse and Hyena and Kitty?)*
                    Love,
                    Tamara
*P.S. This invitation is engraved. See how
hard I pressed with the pen? (Ha ha!)*

"What does noc-turnal mean?"

Realizing Arley had been reading over her shoulder, Dodo crumpled the note and pushed past him into the living room. "It means none of your business."

"Really," he kept up, following her. "What does it mean?"

"What does what mean?" Aunt Hazel asked, laying down a pamphlet on Greece. Lately, Dodo had noticed her aunt poring through travel brochures, planning her next trip. It was a sure sign that summer was nearing its end.

"Nocturnal," Arley told her.

"Of, or relating to night."

"And what's a nocturnal animal?"

"One that is awake and active at night."

"Why would an animal be that way?"

134

Dodo groaned. "Sometimes you're dense, Arley. Do you know that?"

"Then you tell me, smartie," he challenged. "Why would an animal be nocturnal?"

"To hunt at night and surprise its prey. Right, Aunt Hazel?"

"Yes. And some animals are nocturnal in order to find food when their predators are asleep."

"You were only half right," Arley said to Dodo, but his smugness was lost on her. She was thinking about Darwin.

"Are there any nocturnal birds, Aunt Hazel?"

"Of course. Owls come first to mind. They hunt at night and sleep in the day, with the exception of the snowy owl. An arctic dweller, the snowy owl hunts during the day, blending in with the dazzling white of the tundra—"

"Aren't you going to ask?" Arley interrupted.

"What?" asked Aunt Hazel.

"I meant Dodo," Arley explained. "She's got to get your permission to go shopping with Tamara and sleep over her house."

"Is that so?" Aunt Hazel asked Dodo.

Dodo wondered at her own indecision. Two months ago, she would have jumped at the chance to be the Big Fourth. But she hadn't known, then, what the Big Three were really like. She had imagined them as one, vague unit—all for one and one for all, like the Three Musketeers. They were real people, though, with individual personalities. Their friendship worked for them the same way their dancing did. They knew the steps, played their parts. Dodo wasn't sure she had a role in their routine, wasn't sure she even wanted one.

Realizing both Arley and Aunt Hazel were waiting for her answer, Dodo spoke lightly. "Actually, I think I'll skip the shopping part, in case it clears up and we can go down to the bay. But if it's okay with you, Aunt Hazel, I will have dinner with Tamara and sleep over. I wouldn't want to hurt her feelings."

Aunt Hazel sniffed. "Sleepover! A misnamed activity, in my opinion. I'll let you go on one condition."

Expecting to promise to log in a healthy eight hours of sleep, Dodo waited.

"You must reciprocate the hospitality. I'll expect you to ask Tamara to sleep over here one night."

Dodo threw her arms around her aunt, who looked surprised. "What's all this about?"

"It's for having such a good idea," Dodo told her.

"What's so good about it?" Arley wondered out loud. "I hope no one expects me to give up *my* bed."

CHAPTER 16

>———<

SURVIVAL
OF
THE FATTEST

"Listen," Dodo said to Arley and Tamara the next day. They'd left for the bay beach as soon as Mr. Hughes had driven off with Barbie and Gigi. "I've got it figured out. If Darwin goes to sleep three hours earlier every night, in four days his sleeping pattern will be completely turned around."

"You want him to go to bed at nine A.M.?" Tamara asked after she'd spent a moment counting on her fingers.

Stifling a yawn, Dodo nodded. At three that morning, she'd given in to exhaustion and had curled up on a blanket. As far as she knew, Tamara, Barbie, and Gigi hadn't been to bed at all. "And to get up at six P.M.," she went on. "That way, if we can find him a really secure place to live, Darwin will be safe from most other animals. People, too. The only thing left to figure out will be what he can eat all winter."

Since there was no sign of the bird in the drainage pipe, which was gushing with runoff from the streets, Arley suggested that they head for the back of Davy Jones's Locker. As they walked, he pulled a stick off a dead bush and began using it as a scythe, mowing down reeds.

"Oh, no," he said, dropping to his knees at the high tide mark with a frown on his face.

"What is it?" Dodo asked.

"I found my purple sea glass again. Only it's not sea glass. It's still sharp."

Dodo grimaced. "Is that all? Throw it away."

"It's just as sharp as it was weeks ago," Arley said, picking it up to lay it on his palm. "And now there's not enough summer left. Not to erode it the way I want it, anyway."

Dodo bent down to have a look. As far as she could see, the glass had not changed at all. "I guess some things aren't made to order," she said, more gently. "Throw it away so that no one will get hurt stepping on it."

Arley straightened and went over to the slope, where he dug a small hole with the end of his stick. Shoving the purple glass inside, he covered the hole again and marked the place with a large pebble from the beach.

"It's like burying a dream," Tamara said, and she began a funeral march in a high falsetto. *"Pray for the dead and the dead will pray for you!"*

Arley looked at her sternly. "What are you talking about? I'm going to dig it up next summer. By then, it will be something new: dirt glass!"

The girls groaned in unison.

"Come on," Arley flashed, as if they had been the ones taking a break. "If we don't hurry up, Darwin will be in Davy Jones's Locker ordering his lunch!"

The tide was moving out. Before they had walked too far, the path veered away from the slope and began to be cut by small rills of water.

Arley raised an arm to point to an area thick with cattails. "There's a big tidal pool up that way. If we follow this gully, we'll come up behind the restaurants."

The route Arley had indicated was narrow. Dodo went first. Anxious to see Darwin, she picked up speed, first trotting and then galloping under a canopy of fringed cattails standing seven and eight feet tall. When she emerged into the open, she found herself at the base of a retaining wall where several large metal Dumpsters sat. From one emanated several thumps, a scrape, and a happy "Ahhhh."

Dodo climbed easily up the Dumpster's ridged side. She found the dodo munching on half a hamburger. "You make it all right through the storm, Darwin?"

"Oh, hi!" he greeted her. "Want some french fries? There's ketchup here, too. I found a brand-new packet."

Dodo smiled her relief to Tamara and Arley, who were climbing up beside her.

"What an awful lot of food," Tamara said.

Arley leaned forward, laying his stomach on the lip of the Dumpster. As his feet rose, Dodo grabbed the back of his T-shirt to keep him from falling in. "Well, think how many times you've left food on your plate in a restaurant, Tamara. That's what this is, you know. It's the garbage from the restaurants. Is this a Twinkle Pie, Darwin? Oh, no. Sorry. It's a piece of regular pie."

"I hardly ever finish all my food," Tamara admitted. "Unless it's dessert. I always eat dessert."

"Somebody didn't," Dodo observed, watching Darwin gobble up the pastry Arley had tossed him.

"Dessert and a whole lot more," Tamara agreed.

Darwin walked as far up the heap of garbage as he could. Then, hooking his bill onto the container's lip, he pulled himself up to scramble onto the dirt at the top of the retaining wall. Dodo realized then that his main strength lay in his jaw, a part she had never attempted to exercise.

"I'm stuffed," Darwin announced. "I don't think I've ever been so happy in my life! You aren't going to make me go back to that pipe and eat mulberries again, are you? I want to live here."

Jumping to the ground, Dodo wiped her hands on her shorts. "If we can find you someplace safe to sleep, you can stay here. But you have to promise to eat a little more sensibly, Darwin. Have a hamburger but look for some salad and fruit, too. You won't be able to climb in and out of the garbage

140

containers if you get too heavy, you know. Survival of the fittest!"

"Sure you don't mean survival of the fattest?" Tamara suggested, surveying the bird's girth.

Arley was disgusted. "You two are so picky! Darwin won't need to eat so much when he realizes he can have what he wants. Back in the drainage pipe, he had to ration himself. I don't blame him for going a little crazy at first, with all this great food."

"The pie *was* pretty good," Darwin admitted. "Even if it wasn't a Twinkle Pie."

Access to the garbage containers came from a driveway running beside the building. Following it, the children reached a place where they could step up to the ground where Darwin stood.

"We need to do some talking," Dodo told the bird. "I've had a great idea about how you should sleep."

The bird shifted his gaze to the ground, looking sheepish. "I guess you can tell I didn't get much last night."

Arley nodded sympathetically. "The rain keep you up?"

"No. The TV."

All three children spoke at once. *"TV?"*

Before explaining himself, Darwin led the way through some tall weeds. It was obvious that the area between the retaining wall and the back of Davy Jones's Locker was not used. Besides being overgrown, it was littered with old packing crates, discarded chairs, and a broken-up air conditioner. "You see," Darwin said, "I was looking for some-place dry when I found this empty room."

Arley thumped on the silver wall of a large metal box that had been mounted on the building. "This used to be for that air-conditioning unit, over there."

"That's what I figured," Darwin said. When he pecked at it, one side of the box came unhinged, revealing an empty space and a window.

Tamara cocked her head to the side. "Maybe I'm just half asleep, but isn't that window awfully close to the ground?"

"We're on a little hill," Arley said. "The restaurant is built into it."

As Darwin eased into the metal box, his voice echoed hollowly. "What do you think? Available with everything shown here. Batteries not included."

Testing first to make sure the shell would hold her weight, Dodo squeezed in behind him. "It's cozy," she confirmed. "I can see through this window. There's the TV over the counter."

"They play it nice and loud," Darwin told her, "Just the way I like it."

"Can anyone see you, Dodo?" Tamara asked.

Dodo stuck her head back outside. "The restaurant seems empty now, but even if it wasn't, I don't think anybody could. The glass, except for one pane, is frosted. And you know, although it's easy to see things in a lighted room when you're in the dark, it's almost impossible to see things the other way around." She grabbed the loose side of the box and pulled it closed. Though her voice was muffled, Arley and Tamara could hear what she said.

"Do you think you could live in here, Darwin? Do you think you could eat out of the bins at night and sleep here during the day?"

The bird's answer was quick. "And I could watch TV!"

"Give us a turn, too, Dodo," Arley complained, rapping on the box.

Dodo tumbled into the open, fanning herself with her hands. "Be my guest. It's hot in there. I suppose it's the sun on the metal. At least Darwin should stay pretty warm all winter."

"We can leave him the couch cushion he ripped up," Arley said, climbing inside. "Aunt Hazel's only going to throw it out. It'll be like a big, insulated nest. Hey! This is great! Somebody just turned on the TV, and they're watching 'Hospital Zone'!"

"On Sunday?" Tamara asked skeptically. "I didn't think the restaurant would even be open."

"Seven days a week, year round," Dodo said, remembering the sign.

"Oh. You're right," Arley announced. "It was a commercial. But at least they've got it tuned to the right channel."

Not interested in the talk show that appeared on

the screen, Darwin squeezed past Arley. Dodo explained her sleeping plan to him.

"So you see, you'll be much safer," she finished.

"As safe as any animal is."

"And if you forget or need anything after we're gone," Arley told the bird, "just call us. There's a public phone on the boardwalk out front. Only don't use it in broad daylight. Wait until everything is closed, say three o'clock in the morning. . . ."

"Give him my phone number, too," Tamara told Dodo, who had produced her pad and was busy writing. "And we'd better leave him some quarters."

Taking the paper and the money, Darwin tucked them into a corner of his hideaway. "You will come back," he said. "I mean, after the reruns start, you'll come here again?"

"You can count on me," Arley said.

"On me, too," Dodo added.

Tamara shook her head as a thought occurred to her. "Just imagine. When we come back, Dodo, we'll be ready for seventh grade!"

"Please! I'm not sure I'm ready for sixth," Dodo said.

"Who is?"

Arley jumped from Darwin's new house. "No more talk about school. Let's do something."

"I know," Dodo said. "Let's go back to the tidal pool. I saw some sea lavender in bloom. Aunt Hazel said we could dry some and take it home with us."

Arley tagged after the girls. "Did you notice any sea glass?"

"No," Dodo called back, "but I did see the empty shell of a horseshoe crab."

"What's a horseshoe crab?" Darwin asked, bringing up the rear. "You won't expect me to eat it, will you? Hey! Wait for me!"